Governess

....

Barbara Shennen

Copyright © 2024 by Barbara Shennen

All rights reserved.

No portion of this book may be reproduced in any form without written permission from the publisher or author, except as permitted by U.S. copyright law.

Contents

1. Chapter One — 1
2. Chapter Two — 7
3. Chapter Three — 16
4. Chapter Four — 20
5. Chapter Five — 31
6. Chapter Six — 42
7. Chapter Seven — 52
8. Chapter Eight — 63
9. Chapter Nine — 70
10. Chapter Ten — 84
11. Chapter Eleven — 98
12. Chapter Twelve — 111
13. Chapter Thirteen — 118
14. Chapter Fourteen — 140
15. Chapter Fifteen — 146

16. Chapter Sixteen 154
17. Chapter Seventeen 169
18. Chapter Eighteen 177
19. Chapter Nineteen 185
20. Chapter Twenty 193
21. Chapter Twenty-One 201

Chapter One

She ran through the maze, with hedges on either side, laughing. Violet's fists tightly clung to her muslin skirts and her eyes watched the tiny feet that pitter-pattered in front of her.

"I will catch you!" she cried, smiling. The small child squealed in response, and fastened the pace of his little feet. They turned a corner in the maze, without a thought of where they were going. All that was on their minds was to run as fast as they could.

Unfortunately, such childish games are often followed by consequences. The little boy's feet were now running too fast for his body. Within a moment's breath, he toppled face-first onto the ground beneath him, while his little feet laid solitary.

"Fredric!" cried Violet. She stopped at his side and crouched down to his aid. Fredric, though at the impressive age of four, who usually prided himself on being generally tough, now burst into tears. Violet scooped the crippled boy up into her arms and comforted him. Fredric's sobs were muffled as he rested his face against her chest. Violet could feel the bodice of her dress become spotted with wet tears. A tinge of panic filled her stomach; she prayed nothing was terribly wrong with him.

"There, there, Freddy," she said. "Let me have a look at you."

Fredric leaned back enough for Violet to examine his face. He sported a red cut on his left cheek, which Violet gently rubbed with the end of her apron.

"Just a little cut," Violet said in a light tone, trying to smile slightly. Fredric then lifted his palms to show her the scrapes he bore on them. Violet held each hand and wiped away the pebbles that had embedded themselves in his skin when he had fallen. Fredric's cries subsided, until no tears fell from his cheeks any longer. He rubbed his wet eyes with the back of his hand.

"Now, let's get you cleaned up before your Mama sees you," Violet said. Fredric nodded and took his governess's hand.

"How do we get out of the maze?" he asked. Ah yes, where were they in the maze? The hedges that surrounded them were several feet above Violet's head, preventing her from being able to easily determine their exit strategy. She looked back and forth at the possibilities for pathways and chose one at random.

"I believe it is this way," Violet said, with some level of confidence, and led her little student down the path. It took them a few minutes of backtracking and quick decision-making, but eventually the two found their way out of the maze. However, their greatest challenge was inside the Langley Estate. Violet had to get to the kitchen and clean up little Freddy before his mother saw him. Mrs. Langley was a woman very much concerned with appearances, and Violet feared her reaction Freddy's scrapes, dirty clothes, and overall disheveled look.

Violet held Fredric's small hand firmly as they walked down the corridor, about to turn the corner. If she could just clean him up before--

"Ah, Violet, there you are," said a voice from behind. The familiar high-pitched voice made Violent shudder silently. She turned on her heel to face Mrs. Langley.

The lady of the house had a tall, slim figure, and could be considered handsome by some. It was well-known that Mr. Langley married her not for her beauty or her countenance, but rather the heavy dowry which came paired with Katherine Langley, née Parks.

At the sight of her slightly disheveled child, Mrs. Langley's eyes widened in disgust.

"Good heavens! What on earth has happened to you Fredric?"

Fredric looked from Violet to his Mama, and said with spirited enthusiasm, "Violet and I were playing catch in the garden maze. It was awfully fun until I got hurt."

Mrs. Langley's sharp eyes fixed themselves on Violet.

"Violet, you know how I feel about you letting the children run wild in the gardens. Mr. Langley and I employ you to educate Charlotte and Fredric, which is something that cannot be done if you are running around, playing games."

"Now Katherine, you cannot be serious. I believe that out-of-door activities and exercise to do wonders for the mind," a deep voice interjected, startling both Violet and Mrs. Langley. The two turned their heads as a young man approached them. He was even taller than Mrs. Langley, and Violet reckoned, extremely attractive.

Katherine Langley was not a woman to lose her words, but now she struggled to find a proper response. Her long, slender lips curled up into a smile and she chuckled with little sincerity.

"Oh Mr. Langley, what a surprise! We were not expecting you until tomorrow," she said finally. Violet furrowed her brows. Langley? This certainly was not Alfred Langley, Mrs. Langley's husband, so could it be his brother? Violet had never heard a brother mentioned by either of her employers, but it was quite possible. She examined the young man, and found his dark floppy hair to differ greatly from Alfred Langley, which was shorter and greyed. And this man's jawline was quite square and sharp, while Alfred Langley's was narrowed and rounded. And this man's eyes--

Well, his eyes were looking right at Violet's, causing her to blush and look away. She was not used to being around attractive young men. Living at the Langley estate as a governess tended to prevent such things.

He looked back at Mrs. Langley.

"I was able to finish my business early, and thus come here. I hope my being here is not an inconvenience."

"Oh of course not!" cried Mrs. Langley, with another thin-lipped smile, this time paired with the fluttering of her eyelashes. This overly friendly behavior put on by Mrs. Langley was quite unnatural, Violet thought.

"Uncle, uncle, look at my cut!" said Fredric, pointing to the scrape on his cheek. Little Freddy no longer seemed upset by the wound, nor proud necessarily, but he did seem pleased to show it off. Both Violet and Mrs. Langley stiffened.

The younger Mr. Langley validated Fredric's scrapes, and remarked on how he missed seeing his niece and nephew.

"Where is the lovely Charlotte, anyway?" he asked. Violet glanced at Mrs. Langley only briefly before daring to speak.

"She is in the garden drawing the flowers," said Violet softly.

"How lovely. And you must be...?"

"The governess," answered Mrs. Langley. "Now do go on and make Fredric presentable." The latter comment was directed at Violet.

Violet nodded and curtsied. She took one last look at Mr. Langley before whisking little Fredric away.

*

Later that evening, come super time, Violet made her way to the kitchen. She was tired and hungry after the day she had. It took a particularly long time helping Charlotte with her sums--arithmetic was not a favorite of either female--and the stress of Mrs. Langley's wrath was never a joy.

But alas, the day was almost over, and Violet could retire to her room. On her way, she passed by the servant's hall, which was bustling with laughter and chatter. All of the servants were gathered together for super, as they did every night. Violet used to be envious of them, having each other to pass the time with. But she eventually got used to the solitude of her position. Being a governess meant that she was not quite family, get not so low in status as a typical servant of the house. Which meant Violet dined alone in her room. She was used to this arrangement, but some days the loneliness felt heavy.

Still, Violet, would have passed the servant's hall and continued on her way any other day. However, it was the the mention of an "Edmund Langley" by one of the servants that caught her interest. Despite her better judgement, Violet stopped walking a few paces past the doorway to the hall.

"Edmund Langley's arrival will certainly make life interesting for a while," a servant said, Violet couldn't tell which one by just his voice.

"How long is he staying anyway?"

"How do you suppose I know?"

Other servants began to comment on the subject. Their overlapping voices made it difficult for Violet to make out what they were saying. She was about to leave when she heard Mrs. Langley's lady's maid say, "I hear Edmund Langley is studying to be a physician in medical school. Mrs. Langley speaks highly of him,"

"Did you get a look at him? He's incredibly handsome," a female servant remarked. Just then, a two servants exited the servant's hall giggling, and whispering to one another, but they stopped short when they saw Violet. They were all quiet politeness, giving Violet a slight smile and curtsey before passing her and resuming their giddy correspondence. Remembering her place, Violet quickly shuffled away and into her room. What was she thinking eavesdropping on the servants? What had gotten into her?

Violet unpinned her apron from her grey dress and tossed it aside. She had to amit, the intrigue of a young gentleman living among her exited her. Of course she probably would never speak to him after today, and Violet was content with that. Her place was with the children and that was all. But she had to admit she looked forward to having a new face at the Langley estate, even if it was just for a short while.

Chapter Two

The next morning came like any other; Violet readied herself for the day and gathered the children for their morning lessons. Mrs. Langley did not care to be distracted by the children's studying, so they often did their lessons in a small drawing room, turned school room, away from the main part of the house.

Violet clapped her hands to gain the attention of little Freddy and Charlotte, who were still rubbing their eyes from the early morning.

"It is time to work on our letters, children. Please take out your chalk and slates," Violet said. Charlotte, with her long golden hair tied back with a ribbon, replied confidently, "I already know my letters, Miss Violet. I am six, after all."

"I know, dearest. You will be practicing the words we've been working on," Violet replied with a smile. Then she turned to Fredric, "Freddy, you will write your name ten times before we work on writing all of the letters in the alphabet." Freddy nodded enthusiastically and grabbed a small piece of white chalk.

"Watch me draw my name, Miss Violet," said Fredric with bright eyes. Violet nodded and sat next to him at his small chestnut writing table. Her small student drew a long, unsteady line on his slate, as he began to write 'F'. Violet watched proudly as her little Fredric wrote his name with great focus, needing coaching in only a few places. Though she had been governess to Charlotte for two years now, it had only been a few months since she started teaching Freddy, who up until being four, had been cared for by a nursemaid. But Violet already loved him, and his constant enthusiasm for learning and adventure.

"Miss Violet, I--I think I need your help," said Charlotte reluctantly, who was sitting nearby.

"Keep writing Fredric, you're doing wonderful," Violet said, before moving to Charlotte. Headstrong Charlotte, who disliked needing help with anything related to the written language. Charlotte's ambition in life, even at this young age, was to one day become a famous novelist. Of course at the moment, she could barely read and write, but Charlotte took pride in the little she was proficient in. Violet sometimes feared Charlotte put too much pressure on herself to be perfect academically. She knew in her heart no matter what, Charlotte had great potential.

"I'm having difficulties with writing this word," Charlotte said to Violet, pointing to one of the words Violet had written for her to copy. "I can't get it right." Charlotte bit her bottom lip and squeezed the chalk in her hand. Signs she was becoming frustrated with herself.

"That is perfectly normal to have difficulties," Violet said. She put her hand on Charlotte's small back and gave it a gentle rub. "Let's work on this together."

The two began writing, and Violet became so focused on helping Charlotte, that she didn't even notice Edmund Langley enter the room. He stood quietly at the doorway, dark eyes steadfast on Violet. Finally, Violet looked up and noticed him staring. He almost looked distant, as if he were deep in thought. When they locked eyes, however, this changed, and he suddenly became aware of his own presence within the room.

"I apologize for intruding, I--

"Oh, no. It is no intrusion at all," said Violet, rising from her seat.

"I don't believe we had a proper introduction yesterday. I am Edmund Langley,"

"Yes, I know," said Violet. Mr. Langley's rather surprised expression caused Violet to blush. She had not mean to say that out loud. Hesitant, she added, "I am Violet."

"Yes, I know--the governess," replied Mr. Langley. His playful smile relaxed Violet slightly.

The two stood some distance apart, he still in the doorway, and she next to Charlotte. For but a moment they stood staring silently at each other. Violet tried to find something of interest or politeness to say.

She could not, at the moment.

"I could not help but admire you with Charlotte," said the young Mr. Langley, motioning to his niece. At the mention of her name, Charlotte looked up from her work and smiled brightly at the sight of her uncle.

"Uncle, come look at my writing!" cried Charlotte. Before moving, Mr. Langley glanced at Violet, as if waiting for some form of permission to go to his niece.

"Please, do come in," Violet said. She moved away from Charlotte as Mr. Langley approached, bending over to examine the writing on his niece's slate.

Violet could feel her breath quicken and her palms begin to sweat. The mere presence of this young gentleman made her quite nervous. She hadn't realized how very unused she was to that of his sex. And in all her nerves, she hadn't truly heard what Mr. Langley had last said until now.

"You were admiring me?" Violet asked softly. She immediately regretted asking the question as the words left her lips, but it was too late. Mr. Langley had heard them. He straightened, no longer focused on little Charlotte's work. Now his focus was on Violet.

"Yes, I was admiring your patience and kindness with my niece," he said with a friendly smile.

"The children make it easy to be so. They are wonderful children," Violet replied.

"Yes, indeed," said Mr. Langley. He took a few steps closer to her, though he was still a respectable distance away. "I was quite fond of my governess as a child, though I reckon I did not make teaching me an easy feat."

Violet only smiled. She was a little surprised that Mr. Langley was making conversation with her. She was just the help, after all.

"Tell me, where did you receive such an education to be a governess?" Mr. Langley asked. His warm eyes seemed genuinely interested in the answer.

"I was educated by my father, before he passed. He greatly valued education, so he ensured I learned all that I could,"

"That is admirable," said Mr. Langley softly.

Suddenly a servant appeared in a the hallway, looking somewhat frantic; stray wisps of her auburn hair escaped from her white cap.

"Mr. Langley, sir, Mrs. Langley would like to see you in the parlor." she said, before giving him a curtsy and disappearing back into the shadows.

Mr. Langley turned back to Violet.

"Well, I best be going," he said. Violet gave him a silent nod in response. He bowed slightly, she curtsied, and then Edmund Langley left as suddenly as he had entered.

Violet stood motionless for a moment. How strange. She was trying to figure out why the brother of her master had pointedly conversed with her--the help. She scoured for an answer of some ration, but no answer seemed quite right. Edmund Langley was certainly not like Alfred Langley, who found little pleasure in speaking to others, not discluding his wife.

Yes, how very strange indeed.

The sound of Fredric's voice pulled Violet from her thoughts. She quickly resumed her duties as governess, but for the rest of the day, her mind had become heavy with thoughts of Edmund Langley.

*

Sunday came, and along with it, a trip to church with the Langleys. Violet sat with the children during service. Her eyeliner was blocked by the back of Edmund Langley head, who was sitting with his brother and sister in-law in the piew in front of Violet and the children. Because it Violet's duty as the governess, to teach the children religion and morality, Alfred Langley much preferred the children to sit separately with her. Though, Violet often wondered if his preferences actually originated from his distaste for being with his children. Perhaps it was his distaste for people in general.

Violet could never forget her first day at the Langley estate, when a younger Charlotte ran into her father's study to prove to him her knowledge of the alphabet. Her blonde hair, which was shorter then, bounced this way and that as she approached Mr. Langley excitedly.

"Papa! Papa! Listen to me--

"What are you doing in here?" questioned her father. His tone was sharp, and clipped. Violet, who had approached the study's doorway, had known immediately from his response that she had maken a great mistake. "You are not to come in here, Charlotte. Get out."

"But Papa--

"Get out now!" Mr. Langley snapped. He seemed to tower over his poor daughter, with ice in his hard blue eyes.

"Come Charlotte," Violet had said softly. She remembered how her hands had trembled as she took a step towards the girl and gently took her hand. Mr. Langley had taken a long sip of what looked to be brandy, and then placed himself close to Violet's face.

"Do not ever interrupt me in my study again." He said. There was something behind his words that felt like a threat, or at the least, a warning. They fell on Violet with much power, and would forever make her fear Alfred Langley and his temper. Violet quickly learned that he was to be left alone and obeyed without question, especially when he had been drinking.

"Let us pray," the victor's voice cut into Violet's thoughts and brought her back to the present. She watched Alfred Langley's head bow in prayer, followed by his wife's and his brother's. Violet did the same.

After church, Violet was free of her duties as governess for the rest of the evening, as she was every Sunday. Added to this routine, was getting her weekly wages. She set one shilling aside, then folded the rest into a letter for her mother. Holding the letter in her hands, Violet looked out the window from her bedchamber, and studied the sky. Above her hung threatening dark clouds, which were blanketed in a foggy whiteness. The weather did not look promising, but she had to get her letter to the postmaster.

Violet covered her light brown hair with her bonnet, and loosely tied the ribbon. Then she sheltered her shoulders with her warn cloak, and prayed it would not rain until she returned to the Langley estate.

On her way out, Violet passed a servant, who gave her a silent yet stoney glance. It was her daily reminder that she was not accepted by the servants, though some seemed more indifferent than others. Violet sighed and continued on her way out of doors.

It was a bit of a walk into town, though Violet reckoned she would arrive within the half-hour, as she usually did. She enjoyed these walks of solitude. No children to look after, no Langleys to avoid, and no servants to bother with. She was free and at peace on these walks, even if it was part of a greater duty.

Violet could tasted the water in the air. It smelled fresh and crisp. But it wasn't until she had left her letter in the hands of the postmaster and made her way back home, in which the rain finally came. They came first in tiny dropless, which tapped the brim of Violet's bonnet. But within moments, water fell quickly and viciously. Violet clutched the front of her cloak and quickened her pace, which soon turned into a run. The rain was louder than her own footsteps, soaked through her cloak, into her black frock. By the time she reached the entrance to the Langley estate, Violet was wet through and through. She left small puddles of water on the floor as she walked, and her extremities were already numbingly cold.

"Good heavens!" cried Mrs. Langley, who looked horrified as she approached Violet, with Edmund Langley by her side. "What on earth has happened to you?"

"I was caught in the rain when I sent a letter to the post," said Violet.

"Well now you will likely fall ill, and I'll have no one to look after the children." Mrs. Langley said, her thin lips in a line.

"Really, I am fine," said Violet. Then she sneezed.

"Fine indeed. Oh do keep your distance from me, I do not wish to fall ill," said Mrs. Langley. Then she turned to a nearby footman and said, "Thomas, go fetch the doctor,"

At the mention of a doctor, Edmund Langley intervened. "Surely there is no need to fetch a doctor in this weather. My medical education should be enough for a brief examination,"

Mrs. Langley thought for a moment, then said, "Very well," with one of those smiles apparently reserved for her brother in-law.

"I--

Mrs. Langley cut off any attempt of protest from Violet. "You may use the drawing room to examine her," she said to Mr. Langley, before turning on her heal, as if suddenly disinterested by the whole ordeal. Her footsteps echoed down the hall while Mr. Langley and Violet were somehow left alone together again.

"I advise you get out of your wet overclothes as soon as possible," Mr. Langley said, with honest concern in his voice. Tentatively, Violet took off her bonnet and cloak, and held them in her arms. Mr. Langley looked at the clump of cloth she held, then looked around for a nearby servant. He found one in the same servant who had given Violet a cold look earlier. Violet bit her lip.

"Excuse me, Miss," he called. The servant, who Violet recalled was named--was it Mary?--yes, Mary, quickly approached them. "Will you take Miss Violet's things for her?"

"Of course," Mary said to him, with a sweet smile. When she turned to Violet, however, her smile disappeared. Mary grabbed Violet's things from her hands and scurried away before Violet could so much as give her thanks.

"Now, shall we?" asked Edmund Langley, motioning to the drawing room. Violet took a deep breath and nodded. She wasn't quite sure why, but for some reason Violet's stomach suddenly felt fluttery. As she followed Mr. Langley into the room, she tried to determine whether it was nerves or--Lord help her--excitement. But as the door closed behind her, she reckoned it was best that the matter was not further inquired upon.

Chapter Three

"Please, take a seat on the sofa," said Edmund Langley. Violet did as she was told, but not without vexation. She tried to push all thoughts from her mind as she watched Mr. Langley take off his coat and hang it on the pianoforte, which sat in the corner. He rolled up his white shirt sleeves, which contrasted with his stiff dark vest.

Violet took a deep breath and averted her eyes.

"Alright Miss Violet, let's see how terribly ill you are," Mr. Langley said with a light smile. Violet returned his smile, and began to tightly twist her fingers together in the lap of her still damp dress. Mr. Langley approached her and held out his hands close to her jaw. They hovered before her skin, awaiting to touch her, but before they did, Mr. Langley asked, "May I?"

Violet was a bit surprised by the question but she nodded and braced herself for his touch.

Mr. Langley rested his hands on either side of her neck, with his thumbs propped by Violet's jaw line. Violet was surprised by the warmth of his touch, and the gentleness which came from his strong hands. Her breath quickened.

Silently, Mr. Langley tilted her head up, and stared into her eyes, squinting slightly. He pressed his fingers into her skin. "No swollen glands," he said. "Open your mouth."

Violet parted her lips, which stuck slightly together from the sudden dryness of her mouth. Mr. Langley leaned over a bit, as he looked in her mouth. Violet noticed that in Mr. Langley's focused eyes, a wrinkle formed in between his brows. She fixated on that wrinkle, as if to distract herself from how close the rest of him was to her. She had never really been touched by a man before, and though Violet knew these touches were strictly professional, she still could not help feeling affected by them. Violet's only hope was that Mr. Langley could not hear the pounding of her heart banging against her rib cage, for it was all she herself could hear.

"You spoil me, Miss Violet," Mr. Langley said, drawing his hands away from Violet's face. Then, he gently took her left hand and turned her palm upwards.

"How so?" Violet asked. Her eyes darted from her upturned palm to Mr. Langley's face, half hidden by dark tendrils of hair which fell upon his face.

"It is not often I get to examine a real patient like you. Unfortunately medical school surrounds mostly the reading of textbooks and theoretical musings," Mr. Langley said, looking up at Violet. "So I appreciate your indulgence." He then put two fingers on her wrist and studied his pocket watch. "Pulse is a little fast, but normal. I believe you shall be fine, Miss Violet."

"I have not caught my death in the rain, then?" Violet asked, with a surprising hint of cheek. Mr. Langley laughed and stepped back.

"No, certainly not. Though I recommend you put on a dry frock and sit by the fire for a while. The warmth should take that shivering away."

"Thank you, Mr. Langley," Violet said, rising from her seat on the sofa. "Though I feel as though I should call you Dr. Langley, now."

"Hopefully you will in two years time," Mr. Langley said with a chuckle. The two exited the drawing room, and before Mr. Langley had the chance to say anything else, Violet darked away. She walked just slow enough to still be considered to be walking, with the speed of a light jog. She desperately needed to be alone with her thoughts and prayers. There, her confusing feelings surrounding Mr. Langley could be put to rest, now that he would no longer be in such close proximity to her.

Violet closed the door to her bedchambers behind her, and she leaned back against the smooth oak surface. Still gripping the round door knob behind her, Violet rested the crown of her head on the door and closed her eyes. She took a deep breath to relax herself.

Violet could not deny being slightly attracted to Edmund Langley. He was an undeniably attractive man, that even a young spinster like herself could not ignore. Whatever anxiety or miniscule pleasure she found in his presence was completely and utterly due to Violet's lack of familiarity with those of his sex and appearance.

Yes, that was the reason. She was almost certain that if any other young, handsome gentleman interacted with her as Mr. Langley had, she would feel the same way. Right?

Violet rubbed her face with tired eyes and walked further into her small bed chamber. She told herself silently that had likely been the last time she would ever speak to Mr. Langley, as their contrasting stations dictated. Of course, Violet had told herself that same thing the very first day she had met him, and she had been wrong then. Still, Violet pushed her feelings and silent worries away. Her room was dark, as it was now late in the evening and the sky was still shadowed by dark clouds. Despite this, Violet did not bother to light any candles. She somehow felt comforted in the darkness as she slipped out of her damp dress and into her nightgown.

Though she hadn't eaten dinner yet, Violet laid in her narrow bed, with the blankets to her chin. It did not matter, however, as she was not hungry. Instead, Violet closed her eyes and tried to ignore her luming thoughts about why she felt so unsettled around Mr. Langley. Her mind drifted to the money she had sent to her mother, and she hoped desperately that it would be enough to get her Mama by for a while.

Chapter Four

The freshness of the morning proved to do wonders for Violet's spirits and nerves. She felt anew, and was quite eager to begin her tutoring of the children. Even on her worst days, she was always able to take comfort in the children, and their spirited cries of "Miss Violet!" every morning when they were reunited. It was as if Charlotte and Fredric had not seen Violet in a fortnight, rather than a night, and it filled Violet with a warmth most indescribable.

Violet had begun the children's studies with writing, per usual. She swiftly bounced from Freddy's letters to Charlotte's words, then back again. A half hour of this passed rather quickly, as it usually did when Violet invested her full attention to her work. Nothing would distract her today.

"Alright children, let's move on to reading," Violet said. She rose and ran her fingers over the spines of books, which rested on the bookshelf of the school room. "I want to introduce you to one of Shakespeare's plays, which I believe you will enjoy. But--I cannot seem to find it."

Violet scanned the books once more, but alas, she could not find the title she was looking for.

"I'll look in the library for it. I'll only be a moment, but Charlotte, you're in charge while I'm gone," Violet said.

"Splendid!" Charlotte said. She smiled widely and her eyes narrowed deviously on Freddy. Though Charlotte was much fairer and prettier than her mother, Violet almost shuddered at their resemblance just then. As she left the children and swiftly walked through the maze of halls which lead to the library, Violet hoped she would not regret leaving Charlotte in charge of her brother. She thought she heard little Charlotte telling Freddy to sit up straight in a very stern, proper tone.

Oh Charlotte.

Within a minute or two Violet had entered the Langley's library. It was one of her favorite places at the Langley estate, second only to the gardens. Each wall was covered in shelves and consequently, books. There was a sliding ladder to reach the higher shelves, and an armoire in the middle of the room to read in. A fireplace on the far left wall exuded a faint smell of crackling smoke, which paired nicely with the overpowering, yet enchanting smell of book.

Violet took a deep breath and smiled to herself. She dragged her fingers across more book spines, searching for the one in her mind's eye. Eventually she spotted it, and her long fingers clutched it tightly, as if afraid the book would slip out of her grip and fly away.

The school room was a ways away from the library, as they were on opposite wings of the house. Violet, rather skilled at walking quickly, began her journey back, but slowed when she heard men yelling in Alfred Langley's study. Their voices were slightly muffled by the closed door, but Violet could still distinguish Alfred and Edmund Langley's voices behind it.

"I can't believe you, Alfred!" shouted Edmund. Violet's feet stopped, refusing to move. She stood just outside the study, and listened, heart pounding, on the brothers' heated conversation. Though she knew it was wrong, Violet couldn't seem to move. Edmund's outburst had caught her attention. He continued, in a more controlled, yet scolding tone, "You have a wife and children!"

"Oh please, Edmund, your scolds are the last thing I need right now," countered Alfred Langley.

"No, apparently it is only my money that you need," said Edmund Langley.

Violet inhaled a sharp breath. She really should leave--get back to the children. This was none of her business.

"Don't pretend you are better than I, Edmund!" Alfred Langley's deep voice echoed through the walls in a white fury. "Don't think I've forgotten what happened at Oxford."

"That was different and you know it. No, Alfred, I am nothing like you, and never will be."

The study door burst open, releasing a red-faced Alfred Langley, looking like a bull that had just escaped his enclosure. Violet jumped back, startled, and in doing so, dropped her book. Alfred Langley, without looking directly at her, commanded, "Get out of my way!" and pushed passed her.

Edmund Langley then appeared from the study. When his eyes landed on Violet, who's grey eyes were wide in dismay, his expression changed from anger to concern.

"Miss Violet," he said, his tone now gentle, though clearly still vexed. "I reckon you heard that."

"Only a litte, I apologize--

"No, it is I who should apologize. Alfred and I don't always see eye-to-eye, and our arguments can get heated," he explained.

Mr. Langey's eyes drifted from Violet's eyes to her feet. "You dropped your book." He stepped closer to Violet and bent down, picking up her book. Instead of handing it back to her, he examined the words on the clothbound book and read them aloud. "A Midsummer Night's Dream."

"I plan to read it to the children. It's one of Shakespeare's lighter plays, and I think Freddy will enjoy the antics of Puck," Violet said. Her words were strung together quickly and one after the other, like pearls on a string.

"The donkey?"

"No, that's Bottom," replied Violet softly. She fiddled with her hands, still processing the scene that had just unfolded.

"Ah yes, that's right," said Mr. Langley. He held out the book to Violet, and when she took it from him, their fingers overlapped slightly. The surprise of his skin touching hers, even just for a moment, was enough to lose Violet's breath. She pulled the book back suddenly, and avoided looking at Mr. Langley, though she still felt his stare on her.

A silence fell between them.

"Well, I must get back to the children. They will be waiting for me," Violet said finally. Mr. Langley opened his mouth as if to speak, but then shut it and nodded. Violet curtsied and hurried back the school room. The past events flashed before her as she left Mr. Langley, and Violet could not help but wonder what it all meant.

What was that fight about between the brothers? It seemed like Alfred Langley needed money, but that didn't make sense, for both he and Mrs. Langley came from wealthy families.

And what happened with Edmund Langley in Oxford? And why could she not stop thinking about how his touch felt on her bare hand?

Violet reckoned she needed to stop listening in on other people's conversations. It really wasn't worth it.

*

Edmund sat across from Katherine Langley wondering when this hellish afternoon tea would end. He had spent less than a week at the Langley estate and each day had to endure tea time with his sister-in-law and her female companions. Alfred was always absent, and Katherine always had some reason for his lack of presence. Edmund was sure today's absence was due to their argument earlier in the day. Alfred had stormed off on his horse soon after and had yet to return. Katherine claimed he had 'business' to attend to in town. Edmund knew such 'business' likely involved a pub and lots of brandy, but he could not say that to her.

"Really Edmund, do eat something. We ladies cannot bear to eat on our lonesome," said Katherine. Her commanding words were hidden by her light tone of voice and thin smile.

"Yes Mr. Langley, you must eat something," giggled one of Katherine's friends--Ms. Hart, was it? The young lady had been batting her eyes and giggling for the entirety of the afternoon, which was becoming quite tiresome.

Edmund glanced at the table of food before him. Biscuits, fairy cakes, and tiny sandwiches plagued his vision and made his stomach churn. Edmund wasn't sure why, but he had no appetite today. Still, to be polite, he took a sandwich and nibbled the corner.

"Very delicious."

Katherine watched in satisfaction, and with something resembling a giggle said, "How you indulge me! I must say Edmund, I have truly enjoyed your company these last few days."

"Well, I appreciate your hospitality, but I am not certain how much longer--

"You know, the Brown's and the Harrington's have left for London, and the Kent's have gone to Bath for the waters," Katherine said, cutting Edmund off. Another one of Katherine's friends began adding to this list, as if these people's names meant anything to Edmund. In the few days that Edmund had been visiting, he had endured endless chatter from Katherine (and her friends), who were seemingly obsessed with societal gossip and the latests fashions from Paris.

"It seems everyone I know is enjoying a holiday, but Alfred refuses to take me anywhere. I. . ."

Edmund's gaze, and attention, for that matter, drifted from that of Katherine Langley to Miss Violet, who he saw out the window. He watched her outside with the children, running this way and that, as Charlotte and Fredric shrieked with delight at the chase. Edmund smiled to himself at the sight. Miss Violet always seemed so nervous and repressed whenever he spoke to her; it was refreshing to watch such a playful side of her.

He watched as she grabbed Fredric from behind and scooped him up in her arms, twirling and laughing. Her brown hair, usually pinned back in a neat bun, was coming undone. Dark curls hung down, now framing her face, while other escaped locks fell down her neck. It was very becoming.

Edmund suddenly got the urge to speak to her. He hoped that the awkwardness of the morning had worn off. Part of him wanted to explain to Miss Violet why he had been yelling at his brother, but he couldn't bring himself to it. Edmund was still processing what Alfred had done himself. The matter was best left untouched, for the moment.

Katherine stopped talking when she finally realized Edmund had stopped listening to her and followed his gaze to the window. She sighed in a most unapproving tone.

"That governess is out playing with the children again. Whatever can I do to get her to stop?"

"I say find a new governess. The Brown's governess just left them, I could inquire if she is still in need of a new family." said one of Katherine's friends--the one with a large mole on her bosom.

"Need I reiterate this conversation with you Katherine? The children need such exercise to keep their minds sharp," chimmed in Edmund, finally drawing his eyes back to his party.

"Oh, I couldn't agree more, Mr. Langley!" said Ms. Hart with another giggle and eye flutter.

Katherine, not wishing to disagree with Edmund, said reluctantly, "I suppose it cannot cause too much harm," Katherine clenched her jaw, but only for a moment. Then she clapped her hands to regain full attention from her companions, who had all been watching Miss Violet out the window. "Now, enough of that. Who would like more tea? Edmund?"

"Actually, if you ladies will excuse me, I think I'll go see how my patient is feeling. Miss Violet took a walk in the rain last evening, and I want to. . . follow up with that." Edmund said, rising from his chair.

"Didn't you say she would be fine?" Katherine asked, eyes narrowing.

"Yes, but just to. . . be completely certain."

Katherine took a sip of her tea. Edmund could tell by the stiffness of her neck she was not pleased, but in all politeness gave him one of her toothless smiles and said "Very well,"

Edmund gave his regards to the other women and bowed. On his way out he thought he heard Ms. Hart grumble, "She looks fine to me," but Edmund did not care. He was finally rid of the empty conversations which so represented afternoon tea.

Edmund took a deep breath of fresh air and let it fill his lungs as he walked out to his brother's gardens. He quickly spotted the slim figure of Miss Violet, who was chasing Fredric and Charlotte around a large oak tree. Edmund quickened his pace and approached. Charlotte was the first to notice him, and when she did she ran to his side with a bright smile.

"Uncle Edmund!" she cried.

"Violet is chasing us!" Fredric shouted, running to the other side of Edmund. When Miss Violet came around the tree and noticed Edmund standing with the children, she stopped short.

"Mr. Langley," she said, breath quickened from the exercise.

"I realized that this morning I hadn't asked you how you were feeling--after yesterday's jaunt in the rain." Edmund said. As he spoke, he watched as Violet changed from her open and playful countenance with the children, to her usual quiet self. She straightened and smoothed her skirts, as if afraid of what might happen if he saw her even the slightest disheveled.

"That is very kind of you, sir. As you determined last night, I am quite well."

"Very good." Edmund said. He felt like a fool standing there. He had interrupted Miss Violet's time with the children, and made a point of seeking her out, all to confirm something he already knew. What was he thinking?

At least it freed him from afternoon tea.

"Uncle, come into the maze with us!" Fredric said with much enthusiasm. Both he and his sister began tugging Edmund's arms forward, with such a surprising force, that his feet had to oblige. Edmund glanced at Miss Violet, looking for some affirmation that she approved. She only smiled sweetly and followed from behind.

The hedge maze was at the center of the Langley's massive gardens, and were consistently kept clipped and shaped. As soon as they entered, Charlotte and Fredric ran ahead, turning this way and that, and quickly disappearing within the hedges. Edmund and Miss Violet were left alone; only the faint shriek or giggle from one of the children up ahead reminded Edmund of their vague presence.

Edmund and Miss Violet walked side by side, though Edmund was sure to keep some distance between them. They walked in silence for a few paces. Edmund studied the bright green hedges, and familiar pathways of the maze. His childhood came flooding back, like a sudden rain storm, quickly soaking him.

"I haven't been in this maze since I was a little boy," Edmund said softly. The statement was more to himself, than any, yet Miss Violet looked up at him with interest. "This was my home as a child." He explained.

"Of course," Miss Violet said, nodding in understanding. "And Mr. Alfred Langley inherited it."

"Yes, when our father passed."

The two fell silent for a moment, as they turned the corner and made their way down a long, narrow path of hedge.

"Were you close with your father?" asked Miss Violet. Edmund shook his head.

"I barely knew him. He died when I was Charlotte's age."

"I'm sorry,"

"Don't be, my father wasn't worth knowing," Edmund muttered. Violet's large grey eyes widened in surprise. He realized how harsh his words must have sounded, and felt the need to explain. He stopped walking and turned to face Miss Violet. She did the same. Looking down at her, Edmund noticed a flush in her cheeks and light sweat on her brow, likely from running about with the children. Still, she looked beautiful, if in her own quiet way.

What was he going to say? Ah, yes. His father.

"From what I know and remember, my father was not the kindest of men. He was-- ill-tempered, and violent at times, and, well. . . let me say only, that drink was his mistress."

"How terrible," said Miss Violet, true empathy in her voice.

"Well, I was lucky enough to escape him, for the most part. Two years after his death, I was sent to boarding school, and have been away ever since, it seems. It was my brother who endured my father's wrath, with him being fifteen years my senior, and who has indeed suffered the consequences."

"I have encountered your brother's temper a few times, and it is not to be reckoned with, to be sure," Miss Violet said. Now it was Edmund's turn to look at Miss Violet with surprised. Miss Violet took his expression for offense of some kind, and in turn began to panic. "I should not have said that, I apologize. I only meant--

"He has never touched you, as he?" Edmund asked, in all seriousness. He had never seen his brother's violence extend to hitting women--men, occasionally, but never a woman. Still, after learning about Alfred's recent vices this morning, anything was possible, Edmund supposed. Miss Violet's utter shock at this question, the expressive shaking of her head, and her exclamation of "No!" comforted Edmund enough to believe his brother had not stooped so low.

"Good," said Edmund. "Good."

Chapter Five

Edmund and Violet stared at each other as another silence overcame them. They stood in the hedge maze, as thoughts of his brother slowly drifted away. It wasn't until now that Edmund had noticed a small freckle which dwelled on the side of Miss Violet's nose. Now that he really had the chance to look, he began to see more and more freckles, which dotted Miss Violet's skin like little stars in the sky. They weren't clustered together like most freckles, but were spread out, as if each one were placed with careful consideration.

Suddenly Fredric leaped out from behind a hedge, causing both Edmund and Miss Violet to startle.

"This way! Come follow me Uncle and Violet!" cried Fredric with excitement. In a blink Fredric had disappeared back behind the shrubbery, leaving Edmund and Miss Violet no choice but to follow. Edmund glanced at Miss Violet who gave him a soft smile. Then, he turned back to the hedges up ahead, and followed Fredric, who had now joined with Charlotte.

As the group found their way through the greenery, Edmund tried not to think about why he felt somewhat drawn to Miss Violet, and was utterly aware of her closeness now more than ever. He really needed to get out of this blasted maze.

Three more minutes and Edmund did escape the walls of the Langey hedge maze. Though he had been through it countless times as a child, it always was a challenge to get through. But alas, he and his companions were out, and once again able to see the massive grounds surrounding them. In the distance, Edmund spotted a black steed riding up the long road to the Langely's estate. He reckoned his brother had finally come back from the pub.

"Look! Papa's home!" said Fredric, pointing to the horse and rider in the distance. Charlotte followed his gaze but said nothing in response. Instead, she turned to her governess and hugged her leg.

"I feel tired," Charlotte said. Miss Violet stroked the girl's yellow hair softly.

"Then let us retire indoors," said Miss Violet. She looked up at Edmund as if wanting to say something, but not quite finding the words to do so.

"I believe it is here that we part ways. It has been a pleasure," Emdund said, bowing. He knew he was going to regret this, but he turned and started towards Alfred and his horse. He took a deep breath as he crossed the grounds and approached his brother. Edmund wasn't nearly as angry as he had been this morning, but he feared that anger was only resting in Alfred's absence. And if Alfred was in his cups, Edmund was quite sure they'd have a repeat of the morning.

"Where have you been?" Edmund asked, in an accusatory tone. He looked up at Alfred, who was still atop his massive steed. Alfred scowled down at his brother.

"I assumed you would have left by now." Alfred remarked, ignoring Edmund's question. He dismounted his horse, landing heavily a few feet away from Edmund. When they were little, Alfred used to overpower him being older and taller, but now that Edmund was a man, he was no longer intimidated by Alfred.

"I asked you a question," pressed Edmund. Alfred handed his horse off to the stable boy and started towards the house. Edmund followed.

"If you must know," started Alfred, his tone sharp. "I was selling some of Katherine's jewelry."

"Does Katherine know you're doing this?"

Alfred stopped short and faced Edmund. His face was serious, but it also looked tired. Edmund noticed Alfred was acquiring more grey hairs seemingly by the day.

"What do you think?" Alfred asked, though it wasn't a question to answer aloud. Edmund knew Alfred wouldn't have told Katherine, because if Katherine knew Alfred was in need of money, he'd have to explain why.

"So you're stealing your wife's things now? That's a new low."

"I was the one who bought them for her, so in a way they were mine anyway. Besides, Katherine won't miss a few necklaces and rings. I've given her more than enough over the years to make her happy."

Alfred turned his back on Edmund and started walking off, as if their conversation was over.

"You're unbelievable, Alfred." Edmund called. His anger, which had been kept dormit the last few hours, was beginning to awaken.

"You know what Edmund, what else do you expect me to do? I have no other alternatives at the moment. And you've made it clear you have no intention of helping me in the matter."

"But surely there must be another way."

"Do you see one? I am trying to mend my sins, and quite frankly if you're not willing to help me do so, then I suggest you leave."

Alfred's words were like a blow to the chest. Edmund's stomach dropped as guilt engulfed him. Perhaps if Alfred wouldn't have had to stoop to such levels if Edmund had agreed to help him out financially. He sighed.

"Give me a few days to think about it. I won't be able to give you all the money you'll need, but I might be able to help you out a little. I just need some time."

Alfred's expression softened the slightest bit, and he nodded his head in a silent thanks. Edmund still wasn't sure he wanted to lend his brother money, but perhaps he was going to have to.

*

Two days had passed since Edmund and Violet had walked in the hedge maze together, and since then, Violet had seen little of him. She told herself it was for the best, especially when she heard footsteps approaching the school room, and it wasn't Edmund to appear in the doorway, but a servant.

No, it was best she hadn't spoken to Edmund lately. That is how it should be. Violet had no place knowing anything about Edmund's life, or enjoying his presence. She already knew too much as it was.

Violet was the governess. She was not Edmund's equal, and thus, shouldn't expect, nor dare hope, to be in his company more than what was appropriate.

Check yourself, Violet. She thought to herself. She needed to stop whatever familiarity she was beginning to feel with Edmund now, before--before--

"A letter for you, miss," Gerald, the footman said, handing Violet a piece of folded paper, and thus, distracting Violet from her thoughts.

"Thank you," she said. Violet immediately recognized the handwriting on the front, and swiftly broke the wax seal. The footman left her alone in the school room, to read the comforting words of her mother.

"My darling Violet, I am, as always, very grateful for the money you've sent me. It has come a long way here at the cottage, but I can only hope you've kept enough for yourself," Violet read. She smiled slightly. "I worry about you, living with the Langley's, with no friends or home of your own. I hope they're still treating you well. If they ever stop treating you well, do come home right away. We'll find a way to manage.

"To speak of better things, I have begun to mend clothing for Mrs. Reed, who is quickly becoming a loyal customer. Her boys seem to rip or grow out of their clothing faster than I can mend them! But it keeps me busy, and I am quite happy to report, I have already collected a sixpence from her. . . . "

As Violet continued to read her mother's letter, tears began to threaten the brim of her eyes. She missed her dear Mama so such, and rarely got to see her. Her Mama's letters were one of the few comforts she had anymore. And even if they contained mundane conversations, as they usually did, Violet cherished them. They were proof that Violet had her own family, though small. And were a reminder to why she became a governess.

In the emptiness and quietness of the school room, Violet allowed her tears to fall gently down her cheeks. They weren't tears of despair, or even sadness. They were tears of another kind.

Loneliness, perhaps. Or simply missing her mother. Or perhaps she was just tired.

When Violet was able to collect herself, she slipped the letter into the pocket of her apron and made her way outside. It was late in the evening, by now. The children were finished with their lessons, and soon it would be time to retire for bed. But as the spring transitioned into summer, Violet enjoyed taking a turn about the gardens at this time of day. When the moon was fighting for his rightful place in the sky, with the sun eventually giving up in defeat. When the stars began to dot the sky, which was not yet black. When the light breeze carried the fragrances of the flowers and all of God's creatures and living things seemed to be at peace. It was the perfect time to be among nature, in Violet's opinion.

She walked along the pathways, admiring the familiar flowers and shrubbery, which grew to her ankles. Her gaze rested on them for some time, in the hopes they would ease her mind. But when her eyes finally lifted back to the wide groomed pathway, she spotted a dark figure in the distance. Though her vision was darkening quickly from the diminishing light, Violet could make out at least that it was a man, and that he was fast approaching.

Violet tightened her shall around her shoulders.

"Miss Violet, what a surprise to see you," said the man. He stood a comfortable distance away, but was close enough to Violet for her to realize it was Edmund Langley.

"Mr. Langley," Violet said. Her heart began to flutter, and she bit her inner lip in response to his presence. "I have not seen you in a few days,"

"Yes, I have been in hiding, in a way. I need to make a significant decision about a particular matter, and have found advantages in the solitude."

"Then, I shall not interrupt you," Violet said. She turned to leave, desperately trying not to converse for too long with Mr. Langley. But he stopped her.

"No please, will you not walk with me for a bit?" asked Mr. Langley. His dark eyes seemed to somehow shine. Instead of giving him an immediate answer, she countered with a question of her own.

"What would Mrs. Langley think if she saw us walking together?" Violet asked. The darkness that was overtaking the sky seemed to be giving Violet more confidence. She waited for Mr. Langley to react. He looked surprised by the question, as he furrowed his brows. But his relaxed countenance did not change.

"I would expect her to think we were simply walking together and enjoying each others' company," Mr. Langley said. Then he added quickly, "But if she were to have a problem with it, I'll take full responsibility."

Mr. Langley"s crooked smile, and the way one corner of his mouth curled up, gave Violet the confidence he was in earnest. Still, she should have declined his offer. But it was easier to nod and stroll through the garden by Mr. Langley's side.

They walked in tandem down the wide gravel pathway, which turned and straightened across the Langley's massive land. Carefully placed shrubbery and flowers caressed the edges of the pathway, enclosing Violet and Mr. Langley in the greenery. The couple were silent in the beginning, but Edmund soon carried the silence away with his words.

"Tell me Miss Violet, do you make a habit of roaming the gardens at this hour?" His tone was playful, as further proven by his small smile. But his eyes stayed heavy on Violet, waiting for an honest response.

"I try to, when I can. I find this time of day to be so tranquil. Being among the trees and the garden is so. . . calming. And beautiful." Violet said. Mr. Langley pulled his gaze away from Violet and scanned his surroundings.

"I can see what you mean," he said.

"Besides, the honeysuckle is at its most fragrant at this time of day. It's my favorite flower." Violet took a deep breath in and tasted the smell of the sweet honeysuckle, which sat nearby.

"And why is that?" asked Mr. Langley.

"Because even though it is a rather obscure looking wildflower, it has the sweetest, most beautiful scent. And what good are flowers if they are not fragrant?"

Mr. Langley smiled sweetly at her, in a way that made Violet blush.

"Well I cannot argue with that," he said. Mr. Langley paused as they walked a few more steps. Then, he said, "You know, these grounds haven't changed a bit since I was a boy. Same flowers, shrubbery, same everything."

"Did you expect them to change?" Violet asked softly. Mr. Langley shrugged slightly.

"I suppose not exactly. Though, I'd like to think that all living things are capable of change over time."

"We are all capable of change, under the right circumstances. But I believe there is a difference between being capable of change and actually changing."

"And you, Miss Violet? Have you changed over time?"

Violet was surprised by Mr. Langley's intimate question. She had never really thought about how she'd changed, but looking back, Violet found it difficult to deny.

"My hopes and ideals have changed, I suppose. My life is much different now, and from that, I believe I have changed."

"And might I ask what those hopes and ideals were?" asked Mr. Langley. It was fortunate that the atmosphere was darkening, for it meant Mr. Langley was unable to see the flush in Violet's cheeks.

Violet knew it was likely best not to answer such a question as that. To talk about her feelings to a man she barely knew, especially Mr. Langley, was less than appropriate. Perhaps it was the night, or even the simple fact that he was the only person to truly show the slightest interest in knowing her. Violet wasn't sure, but it didn't matter. Before she could be rational, the words spilled out of her, as if they had been trying to escape for a long time.

"When I was younger, I dreamed of what every young woman wants--a husband that I loved, and a family of my own. A home to be mistress of," Violet said.

"And that has changed?" Mr. Langley asked, his brows furrowed slightly.

"I don't hope for it as I used to, as I know I'll never have it."

"And why is that?"

Mr. Langley stopped walking, causing Violet to stop as well. They faced each other.

"Because I am a governess now. I am not getting any younger, nor do I have ample opportunities to socialize with men of my age and station."

"Surely there must be some nice lad in the servant's quarters that strikes your fancy," said Mr. Langley. Looking up at him, Violet had not quite realized how much taller Mr. Langley was that her. She barely came to his shoulders, causing her to cran her neck up to look at him.

"The servants are not particularly fond of me." Violet said.

"How can that be?"

"My position as a governess puts me in a slightly higher station than them. Most think I put on airs and am no better than them. Thus it is difficult to become friendly with them ," said Violet. Violet immediately feared she had said too much. She felt her stomach knot and became suddenly aware of how close she was standing to Mr. Langley. Violet looked down and her feet and watched them as they began to move.

"I had no idea," Mr. Langley said softly. "That must be incredibly hard to endure." He stayed by her side while they continued down the lane. Violet should have stopped talking by then, as she had already shared enough. But there was something about Mr. Langley and his questions that made her want to share everything with him. It was not often she found someone wishing to know her.

"As I said, hopes and priorities change. I never thought I'd become a governess, but now that I am one, I have different ambitions." Violet said.

"And what a magnificent governess you are. The children really seem to adore you. Might I ask why you became one?" asked Mr. Langley. Violet bit her bottom lip. She had never explained this to anyone before, and a part of her feared she would be pitied by Mr. Langley if he knew. She looked up at him and hesitated for a moment, but nodded.

"When my father died, a distant male relative inherited nearly everything. My mother and I were left practically destitute. With my education and fondness of children, it seemed the best option was to become a governess," Violet said. "I have food and board, and am able to send what little money I make to my mother. We get by, and with that I must credit the Langley's."

Mr. Langley said very little. His silence was overwhelming, and Violet suddenly feared very much what he thought of her. "Do you pity me, sir?"

"No," replied Mr. Langley, to much Violet's surprise. His eyes widened, for fear of offense and continued, "I only mean that I admire you, more than pity you. I think it is very brave and good of you to work and support your mother. I cannot say I know many ladies who would do such a thing."

"Oh," whispered Violet shyly. She was not used to compliments. "I am only doing what anyone would do for family. We help those we love, do we not?"

Mr. Langley bowed his head slightly, as if deep in thought. After a moment he met Violet's eyes and replied, "I do believe you're right. Thank you, Miss Violet, as you have just help me make that difficult decision I've been trying to make."

"My pleasure," Violet said with an awkward laugh. She did not wish to press what the decision was, but she guessed it involved Alfred Langley.

Violet looked up at the sky, only to discover it had turned black, and the stars were shining like little mirrors in the sun. How did it become nightfall so quickly?

"You must excuse me Mr. Langley, as it has become much too dark. I believe it is time I retire for the night." Violet curtsied.

"Yes, of course," replied Mr. Langley. He opened his mouth as if do say something else, but closed it and gave her a simple nod. Violet turned and made way for the house, and as she walked, she let her shawl grow looser and looser around her arms.

Violet left Mr. Langley standing in the dark gardens, but she knew he would not be leaving her thoughts tonight.

Chapter Six

The next morning came like any other--much too quickly. Violet found her thoughts were overgrown with Mr. Langley, as they had been of late. In the freshness of the new day, she realized just how much she had shared with him last night, and was quite vexed. What had compelled her to be so open and speak so freely? It was rather unlike her. At the same time, she rarely had such an opportunity to speak with another. Could she truly blame herself for finding pleasure in a companion?

Violet wished she could get out of her own mind. Her thoughts and worries were her own folly. Unfortunately, matters were not helped when the servant, Mary appeared in Violet's bed chambers.

"Brought some clean linens," Mary said, holding up her stack of cloth. Violet smiled and gave a remark of thanks. Mary sat the linens on Violet's bureau. Instead of leaving, she strolled casually to Violet's window and looked out, as if it was her own bed chamber she was in.

"Ye know somethin' 'bout the window in the servants' quarters? The one window we've got?" Mary asked, eyes still steadfast on Violet's window, looking out. Violet stood some paces behind her, hands tightly intertwined. This was the most Mary or any other servant had ever said to her, and it was quite unsettling.

"Pray tell," Violet said softly.

"It's got a surprisingly good view of the gardens." Mary turned her head back just enough to make eye contact with Violet. Her eyes were nearly black. It sent shivers down Violet's spine and an almost immediate nausea sensation was triggered.

"How lovely," Violet said, forcing herself to smile. She wasn't quite sure where Mary was going with this conversation, but something told her it wasn't just to make light chit-chat.

"Couldn't help but notice ye and Edmund Langley seemed quite familiar walkin' in the garden last night," Mary said, her cockney accent strong. She turned her back to the window, facing Violet completely. Mary's eyes were narrowed, and she held an arrogance in her countenance that was utterly unappealing.

"We've had a few conversations, but it was nothing more than being friendly." Violet said. She tried desperately to keep her voice steady, and appearance calm, but inside she was sheer panic.

"Is that so? Miss Proper Governess isn't try'n to snag herself a wealthy husband?" questioned Mary. A strand of her black hair had escaped the constraints of her white cap, and hung along her sharp jawline.

"I don't know what you're getting at Mary, but I would prefer it if you would leave."

Mary smiled, as if satisfied by Violet's response. She took a step forward, so her face was only a few inches from Violet's. Mary's eyes drifted up and down Violet, as if sizing her up.

"Ye know he'll never marry someone like ye," Mary sneered. She pushed passed Violet and left the bed chamber with her head held high.

Violet took a deep breath and smoothed her skirts, in the hopes that by doing so, she would collect herself. She couldn't understand why Mary had made such a point of telling Violet she was aware of her. . . friendliness. . . with Mr. Langley. Was she truly just aiming to insult Violet? Violet knew Mary had never liked her, perhaps more so than the other servants. But this visitation was rather malicious.

She knew she should not have walked with Mr. Langley.

*

Violet was still a little shaken by Mary's visit, but what was waiting for her in the school room proved to have more of an effect on her.

Her lessons with Charlotte and Fredric had started with much normalcy. Violet took comfort in the children and their readiness to learn, and had almost forgotten what had happened in the last four and twenty hours. That is, until it was time for their daily reading of 'A Midsummer Night's Dream'.

"Charlotte, will you fetch me the book?" asked Violet, whose lap was preoccupied with Freddy. She rested her chin on the top of Fredric's golden head, her arms wrapped around him. How irrevocably good it felt to snuggle a small child, especially one you loved. Violet watched as Charlotte ran to the book shelf and grabbed the requested book, before handing it off to her.

"Thank you," Violet said. Charlotte took a seat next to Violet and little Freddy, and leaned towards them, for a better view of the book. Violet opened 'A Midsummer Night's Dream', feeling the worn leather with her fingertips, like she had been doing for the last few days. But unlike the last few days, Violet discovered something resting within the pages.

"What is that, Violet?" Charlotte asked.

Laying, pressed between the paper, was a honeysuckle blossom. Violet gently picked up the flower and held it up to inspect. Its long, thin petals stretched out like fingers, and scented the pages with its sweet fragrance.

"It's a honeysuckle flower." Violet said finally, nearly forgetting to answer Charlotte.

"Where did it come from?" asked Fredric.

"I-I don't know."

But Violet did know. Or at least she thought she did. As soon as her eyes had laid upon the pressed honeysuckle, she thought of Mr. Langley, and of their conversation in the Langley garden last night. He was the only person who knew of her partiality to the flower, besides her mother. And it seemed like too much of a coincidence for honeysuckle to be placed carefully in a book Mr. Langley knew she was reading to the children.

Violet smiled to herself. But what did it mean?

"Here, smell it," Violet said, holding the flower to Fredric's nose, then to Charlotte's. Charlotte breathed in and sighed as she let out her air.

"It smells delightful," Charlotte said. "And familiar."

"That's likely because you've smelt it before in your gardens," Violet said with a chuckle.

"Can I have it?" Charlotte's blue eyes were wide and hopeful. Violet took one last look at the little yellow flower and handed it to the girl. She began to read Shakespeare's play to Charlotte and Fredric, but her mind was elsewhere.

Assuming that it was indeed Mr. Langley who had put the honeysuckle in the book, what had prompted him to do so? Violet and Mr. Langley had spoken several times now, and had become somewhat friendly towards one another. But, this gesture seemed to cross the constraints of polite friendliness. Violet was not certain how to feel. She could not deny the quiet pleasure she took in the idea that Mr. Langley had given her a honeysuckle blossom. It made her feel as though someone saw her as more than just a governess.

But wasn't that what Violet was? Just a governess? A governess who should know her place. Who should not be receiving flowers from her employer's family.

As much as Violet hated to admit it, she knew she needed to speak with Mr. Langley. She needed to find clarity within the confusion. But first, she needed courage to talk to him.

While the children dined with their family, Violet paced in her room, hoping to find the right words to say to Mr. Langley. What did she in fact wish to say to him? She strung words together in her mind and played them back to herself. Then she found different words and tried again. Oh, this was hopeless.

After the children finished eating, Violet took them outside. Charlotte was to practice her drawing by using the garden as her muse, and Fredric was to explore nature and collect his discoveries. Little Freddy quickly ran off, likely insearch of some creepy-crawly creatures. Violet kept her eye on him as she directed Charlotte's drawing.

"This part needs shading," Violet told Charlotte. Her vision flickered from Charlotte's drawing to Freddy. However, her vision quickly shifted when she spotted Edmund Langley sitting on a bench in the distance. Now was her chance to speak with him, if she dared. Just at the thought of approaching Mr. Langley, Violet's heart began to race and her palms began to sweat.

Somehow, some way, she managed to excuse herself from Charlotte's side, and walk towards him. Her feet carried her until she was standing over Mr. Langley, who sat reading a book.

Now, as she was in front of Mr. Langley, Violet realized she knew not what to say. She tried to find the words she had practiced in her head, but it was all a blank. At the moment, all Violet could muster was a weak, "Mr. Langley?"

Mr. Langley pulled his gaze away from his book and lifted his head. He smiled when he saw Violet standing there..

"Miss Violet! Forgive me, I did not see you there," he said, standing.

"I apologize for intruding." replied Violet. Her entire upper half became incredibly stiff and her fingers began to tangle themselves together in their oddly comforting way.

"Your presence is never an intrusion."

At those words Violet swallowed hard and took a deep breath. She could do this.

"Mr. Langley, might I ask you a question? A rather frank one, I must add." Violet kept her eyes steadfast on the grass surrounding Mr. Langley's feet, but flickered them to meet his gaze every few breaths.

"Well now I'm intrigued. I'll allow this frank question." Mr. Langley smiled playfully, but the effect it had on Violet was not at its usual strength.

"I... have been wondering, given our differing stations, why--why you have been so friendly towards me? I am only an employee of your family, though you speak with me with--with an openness. . . . as though we are equals."

Had she really said it? Had Violet actually just said that to Mr. Langley? From the bewildered expression his face now possessed, Violet reckoned she had indeed.

"Are we not equals?"

"No," claimed Violet. "I don't believe we are."

Mr. Langley thought for a moment, all quietness. He took a step forward, so that he now stood only a couple of feet away from Violet. It forced her to look up at him. The soft breeze which danced in the air, caught a few of Mr. Langley's locks and pushed them this way and that. It was enough to distract Violet as she waited for a response from Mr. Langley, even if only for a moment. It felt like years, but finally, Mr. Langley replied.

"Well, first, to answer your question--I am friendly with you, simply because I enjoy your company," he started. "You are not like any other woman I've met before. You have a pureness about you, a strength, and are incredibly caring."

Violet felt her cheeks begin to flush.

"I admire you," continued Mr. Langley. He paused again, long enough for Violet to dare look in his warm brown eyes. His irises flickered, as if searching for something in Violet's own large, grey ones.

"And second, I am quite certain that if we are indeed not equals, then surely you must be my superior."

Violet lost all of her words. They escaped her before she was able to speak. Violet had considered what Mr. Langley's response might have been, but none of her guesses had come close to what Mr. Langley had just professed. She wasn't quite sure how to feel about it, though she knew a small part of her was pleased. Or at least flattered.

Mr. Langley looked at her expectantly, waiting for some kind of reply from Violet. But how can one respond to such a statement? Horrifyingly, all Violet was able to manage was a simple, "Oh,"

She filled the space between them with a smile.

"I don't believe your family would approve of me keeping company with you," Violet said. Her voice was but a whisper.

"Must they know?"

Violet considered this. She knew as a governess, she shouldn't step out of her place. But as Violet, she could not say she truly wished to stop talking to Mr. Langley. Would it be so terrible if Katherine and Alfred Langley were not aware?

"No," Violet decided. "I suppose not."

"Then we shall be friends, if only in secret."

Mr. Langley and Violet smiled to one another at this agreement. Violet wasn't at all intendeding for her confrontation with Mr. Langley to end this way. However, she could not say she was sorry it did not end differently.

*

The evening came, and with it Violet's thought felt far away. She kept replaying her conversation with Mr. Langley through her mind. As she walked down the hallway of the Langley estate, everything else seemed to drift away. That was, until, a servant burst from the servant's hall clutching a small case. Tears ran down her face as she walked past Violet. She recognized the servant as Mrs. Langley's lady's maid.

"Whatever is the matter?" Violet asked, stopping the girl by placing her hand on her arm. The maid looked at Violet in utter despair. Her eyes were red and her cheeks were wet.

"Mrs. Langley. Just. Fired me!" the maid cried between gasps of breath.

"Why?"

"She said. I stole from her. Jewelry. But I didn't, I didn't! I never stole nothing in me whole life!" cried the maid. Violet knew not what to say. Though she didn't know the girl very well, her heart still broke for her. Violet knew it would be difficult for the girl to find another position, especially with such a claim held over her. She would likely end up in the poor house, and live the rest of her life in misery. Violet wasn't quite sure how to comfort her, so all she said was, "I'm sorry,", and watched as the maid nodded and continued on her way. The girl was met at the end of the hall by some of her actual friends, each who embraced her, and walked with her to the servant's entrance door. The girl was sobbing as she bid farewell to the other servants. She couldn't have been older than seventeen.

"What has happened?"

Violet looked up, only to find Mr. Langley at her side, watching the scene unfold.

"Mr. Langley, whatever are you doing in the servant's part of the house?" Violet asked, surprised by his presence.

"I heard the most horrid crying and followed the sound," said Mr. Langley. "Poor girl."

Violet looked back at the maid as she slipped through the door and left the Langley's estate.

"That was Mrs. Langley's lady's maid. Mrs. Langley accused her of theft and let her go,"

"Theft of what, exactly?"

"Of Mrs. Langley's jewelry, apparently. But she claims she didn't steal it."

With those words, Violet watched as Mr. Langley's expression changed from concern to anger. He clenched his jaw and took a deep breath.

"Jesus Crist," he muttered under his breath. Mr. Langley, having locked eyes with Violet, quickly excused himself and turned on his heel. Violet watched in confusion as he disappeared around the corner. She wondered where Mr. Langley was going.

Chapter Seven

Edmund burst into his brother's study in a fury. It was becoming a habit of his to do this, and quite frankly, it was getting old. Alfred was sitting behind his desk, cupping a glass of brandy in his overly large hand. Upon entering the room, Edmund shut the door behind him with a little too much force. The sound of the door banging echoed in the small, dark room, causing Alfred to startle. Without so much as a greeting, Edmund began interrogating his elder brother.

"Do you know what Katherine has just done?" Edmund inquired. He stood over his brother, the only thing separating them was the massive desk between them. Disinterested, Alfred took a sip of his brown drink and sighed.

"Likely something I care nothing about," said Alfred. Then he pressed his index finger to his bottom lip and squinted his eyes, as if in deep thought. "But as I am a betting man, let me guess: has she decided to change the wallpaper in the parlor again? Or acquire a new China pattern for our dishes?" Alfred's facetious tone made Edmund's blood boil.

"She has accused her maid of stealing the jewelry that you took."

Edmund waited for some kind of reaction from his brother, but Alfred's countenance was completely unfazed. He took another sip of his drink and set the glass down on the oak desktop.

"How unfortunate."

Edmund stared blankly at Alfred.

"Do do realize the maid has been let go of your staff? Katherine falsely fired a young girl with no money or prospect of a new position."

"As I said, it's unfortunate. What more do you wish me to say?"

Edmund's fists tightened as they propped themselves on Alfred's desk. His knuckles whitened and his shoulders hovered over his brother. Edmund had never had a close relationship with Alfred, but he thought he knew is brother better than this. How could Alfred be so cold-hearted?

"For starters," Edmund spat. "You could tell your wife what really happened to her jewelry, and why you had to pawn it. Then you could re-hire the maid."

At this suggestion, Alfred laughed. Laughed. And rose from his chair.

"You know I cannot do that, Ed."

Edmund clenched his jaw, biting down hard on his teeth. As Alfred strolled across the room to the hearth, Edmund followed him from behind.

"Then perhaps I will," Edmund threatened. This seemed to catch Alfred's attention, causing him to turn around and face his brother.

"Will you, Edmund? Will you really? Have you already forgotten that you owe me?"

"How long will you try to hang that over me, Alfred? Oxford was a long time ago. And I never asked for your help then." A tinge of guilt pricked at Edmund, but he kept his expression hard.

"And yet I gave it. And I know you. You don't have it in you to tattle on me," Alfred said. He took a step closer to Edmund, staring him down like a wild animal, ready to make his kill. "You also know that you do owe me for Oxford, and because of that, I doubt your conscience will allow you to tell Katherine my... folly."

Edmund hated that his brother was right. Deep down, he couldn't expose Alfred. Though the truth of what Alfred had done would come out eventually, if nothing was to be done about his situation. Still, it angered Edmund that Alfred appeared to have no conscience or empathy for the poor maid.

"Perhaps you are right. But that does not change my disgust in you," Edmund said with a sigh of defeat. His eyes were still hard on Alfred, and he wondered how he was going to stomach helping his brother when Alfred clearly did not deserve it.

*

Violet wondered why Mr. Langley had stormed off when he had learned about the lady's maid. But days had passed since then, and Mr. Langley no longer appeared to be so vexed. Part of Violet wondered if his vexation was somehow intertwined with Alfred Langley. She still could not forget overhearing the brothers argue heatedly days ago, but Violet daren't ask about it, or the details behind Mr. Langley's latest upset. Violet still knew her place, even if the edges of 'her place' seemed to be blurred at the moment.

In truth, Violet had been in high spirits since her conversation with Edmund Langley. She still felt conflicted about the whole situation, but whenever she spoke to Mr. Langley, these anxieties seemed to fade away.

Violet smoothed her skirts and entered the school room, expecting to be met by Charlotte and Fredric, as she commonly did every morning. However, the small room was empty, and appeared quite barren without the lively spirits of the children to fill the space.

How odd.

Violet turned on her heal and began searching for the children, next looking in their bed chambers, then their favorite hiding places. She was bent over, draped over the sofa of the drawing room, looking behind it, when Mrs. Langley appeared from behind.

"Good heavens, what on earth are you doing, girl?" Mrs. Langley interrogated. Violet snapped upright and whipped around to face her employer. Her face immediately redded, and her heart began to pound.

"Mrs. Langley!" Violet exclaimed. Her voice was much too high and enthused; a result of anxiety and nerves when in the presence of Mrs. Langley.

"I--the children were not in the school room," explained Violet. Mrs. Langley's eyes narrowed, causing her brows to furrow.

"And your conclusion was that they must behind the sofa?" Mrs. Langley asked. Her tone dripped with judgement and elegant skepticism, a trademark of the great Katherine Langley. Violet, embarrassed, bowed her head and began playing with her fingers.

"Have you--have you any idea where they might be ma'am?"

"I believe knowing where my children are is your job, Miss Violet. Not mine," scoffed Mrs. Langley. Her eyes met Violet's, and they stood staring at each other for nearly two ticks. "Why are you still standing there? Go find my children!"

Mrs. Langley shooed the governess with her long fingers. Violet nodded and scurried out of the room like a mouse having just seen a cat.

"And don't mettle with my furniture in the process!" Mrs. Langley called from the drawing room.

"Yes ma'am!" said Violet.

Violet sighed, and became more frantic as she searched the house with no success of finding the Langley children. When nearly every inch of the massive home was inspected, Violet took to the gardens. She scanned the flat, and very much groomed, land, seeing no sign of her pupils.

Where could they have gone? And what was Mrs. Langley going to do to her if she didn't find Charlotte and Freddy?

Just as Violet was about to turn back to the house, she heard a childlike screech in the distance. Violet stiffened, and listened as she awaited another screech, which did indeed sound a few seconds later. Her heart began to pound, fearing the worst as Violet followed the shrieks. They took her behind the estate, where the gardens consisted more of open field and carefully groomed trees and shrubs. Violet listened.

Screech. Shriek. Giggle. Giggle?

As Violet turned the corner, Charlotte and Fredric came into sight, along with Edmund Langley. Each held a long, thin stick in their hands, which they swung in the air like swords. They laughed and shrieked as their sticks clattered together in battle. Violet let out a breath she knew not she had been holding at the sight of them. She was not certain whether to feel relieved or irritated that Mr. Langley had taken the children without her knowledge.

Violet stood some yards away, watching the three at a close, yet silent distance. Charlotte and Friedric seemed in such felicity as they played with their uncle.

Yes, it was mainly relief that Violet felt. After a few moments, however, she felt the necessity to intervene, despite not wanting to end the children's fun. Violet cleared her throat.

"Eh-hem."

The children and Mr. Langley continued to yield their weapons, having not noticed her. She tried again, a little louder.

"Eh-hem!"

All three turned their heads in her direction at once.

"Miss Violet!" Charlotte and Fredric cried in unison. "We're playing pirates with Uncle Edmund!"

Violet and Mr. Langley's eyes met and they shared a smile. Mr. Langley breathed heavy from the exercise, and his brow glittered with sweat. He wore no overcoat or cravat; his crisp white shirt sleeves were rolled up to his elbows, and his deep brown vest covered much of his waist. Mr. Langley's undone appearance made Violet blush. She realized she had been staring at him for much too long without saying anything. So, Violet turned her attention on the children.

"Children, it is time to begin your lessons for the day," she said in a steady tone. Fredric's expression fell in an instant. His pink lips pouted and his brows furrowed in upset.

"But I want to keep playing!" Fredric whined. As much as Violet enjoyed playing with the children, she knew she needed to begin their lessons, or

Mrs. Langley would have her head. It was bad enough Violet had already lost their whereabouts for nearly a half hour.

"Fredric, you may play after you and Charlotte finish your lessons."

"Please Violet?" asked Charlotte, joining in on the plea. Charlotte approached her governess and looked up at her with those large blue eyes, clutching at Violet's skirts. "Just a few minutes more?"

Violet looked from Charlotte to Fredric, then up at Mr. Langley who shrugged and gave her a small smile.

"Five minutes," Violet commanded at last. "And not a minute more!" The children squealed with happiness and quickly resumed their intense stick battle.

Violet stood watching them, trying desperately not to fixate her attention on Mr. Langley and how the undone buttons at the top of his shirt allowed her to see a peak of his chest hair. Yes, it was best if she kept her eyes focused on the children. But then, Mr. Langley bent down and picked up a second stick.

"Will you not battle with us, Miss Violet?" asked Mr. Langley. He pointed the stick at her, holding it out for Violet to take. At this request, Charlotte and Fredric pleaded Violet join them as well.

"No, thank you. I am quite content watching from a safe distance." Violet said, staring at the stick, which continued to be held out to her.

"No one had any fun watching from a safe distance, I daresay." replied Mr. Langley. Violet looked up at him, and his challenging eyes, which now shone almost amber in the sunlight. Mr. Langley raised his eyebrows, and waved the stick a bit, as if challenging Violet to take it.

Violet glanced back at the house. The servant's window was on the other side of the house, so Mary shouldn't be spying on them. And five minutes surely wouldn't be long enough for anyone else to see them. Violet bit her lip, in consideration. Then she took the stick from Mr. Langley and said, "Oh alright."

Charlotte immediately swung her stick in Violet's direction, but Violet caught the blow with her own stick. Violet giggled, surprised by her abilities. But, remembering Mr. Langley's presence, she stopped herself from any further giggles or smiles. It was not dignified to be seen playing in such a manor by someone like Mr. Langley. She glanced in his direction; he had already resumed a rather intense battle with little Freddy. Charlotte poked Violet in the arm with her stick, causing Violet's attention to be drawn back to the little girl.

"Onguard!" Charlotte cried. Her eyes were narrowed with intensity, yet she bore a rather large smile on her face. Violet was slightly terrified. All worries and thoughts of Mr. Langley's presence drifted away with the wind, as Charlotte began to whack and jab Violet with her stick. Violet had no choice but to defend herself, and quickly became entrapped in their game.

What ensued next was a playfully intense battle between two young children, a governess, and a medical student. Violet was tentative at first, but it did not take long for her to yield her stick with much vigor. Charlotte swung this way and that, and each time her shots were blocked by Violet. As Charlotte continued to advance, Violet took a step back, then another, and another. Suddenly, she felt a warm, strong back against her own. Strong shoulder blades pillowed the back of her head, as her spine felt another's. Violet immediately jumped forward and whirled around, only to find herself face to face with Mr. Langley. The surprise of bumping into him rendered her imobal. She stood there dumbly, staring at him. Even by accident, Violet was quite affected and startled by Mr. Langley's touch. It burned her skin, or was it a tingle?

Mr. Langley gave Violet a light crooked smile, clearly unaffected by their brief contact. However, such a smile distracted Violet enough for Charlotte and Fredric to charge at her, wailing with such a force, they knocked her over. The children's little bodies piled atop Violet's as they giggled and squirmed. Though Charlotte and Fredric were light in weight, the two of them together were quite successful in pinning Violet to the ground, with no hope of escape. All Violet could do was rest her head in the grass and laugh.

"Alright children, I think that's been enough," chuckled Mr. Langley. His face came into view, hovering over Violet. Charlotte crawled off of Violet at her uncle's command, but little Freddy was not so obedient.

"You shan't take my treasure!" the boy cried as his small hands pressed upon Violet's shoulders. Mr. Langley bent over and scooped Fredric into his arms with little effort, before plopping the child next to his sister. Then Mr. Langley turned back to Violet, who was now sitting up, and quite sure there were blades of grass stuck to the back of her arms. He offered his hand to Violet as he looked down at her aimiabley.

Violet's eyes steadied on those strong hands, remembering their touch when she played patient some days ago. She decided to decline his offer of assistance, by silently rising on her own. Mr. Langley's hand fell to his side awkwardly.

"It has been much longer than five minutes, I fear," Violet said. "It is time we retire inside, I reckon."

This time the children obliged to Violet's words, and they slowly made their way to the front of the house. Mr. Langley walked at Violet's side; Violet was utterly aware of his presence. She walked stiffly and quietly, very much unlike her countenance only moments ago.

"I have decided something, Miss Violet," Mr. Langley said, cutting through the silence. His gaze stayed steadfast on the children, who skipped and scurried some distance ahead.

"Is that so?" Violet inquired.

"Yes, well I've been thinking about our conversation that we had some days ago. And I've determined that if we are to become friends of sorts, it is only right you call me by my Christain name."

Before Violet could protest on the grounds of impropriety, Mr. Langley quickly added, "Only in private, of course."

Violet pondered this thought. She had wondered how simply 'Edmund' would taste on her lips. It was such an act of familiarity, to call him by his first name. She had never done such a thing before, and ought not to now, but Violet could not help but agree to it.

"Then, I insist you call me just 'Violet' in private." she said. Mr. Langley, or, rather, Edmund, smiled in great satisfaction.

"Alright, just Violet."

The two exchanged a sweet look, which solidified their agreement. The moment, however, did not last long, due to the sudden appearance of a narrow-eyed Mrs. Langley.

"Mrs. Langley!" Violet said, tearing her eyes away from Edmund.

"Katherine!" Edmund exclaimed.

"I see you've finally found the children," Mrs. Langley said to Violet, in a tone that was most ungrateful. She glanced at her children, who were now running around the gardens. Violet followed the woman's gaze.

"Yes, indeed. They were enjoying time with Mr. Langley."

Violet's heart pounded, so much that she felt its vibrations in her ears.

Boom-boom. Boom-boom.

Had Mrs. Langley seen her playing most inappropriately with Edmund and the children? No, Violet doubted it. But, it was a close call.

"And now they are not. So, Miss Violet, should you not be tutoring my children at this moment? Rather than standing here, loitering in my gardens?"

"Oh-yes, I was just about to--"

"Go then!" commanded Mrs. Langley. Her voice was not raised in the least, but her tone was quite serious. Mrs. Langley possessed such a talent of never seeming quite interested enough to raise her voice, yet she easily commanded a room. It intimidated Violet greatly.

"Yes ma'am." Violet said. She dipped her head in a quick curtsy before glancing at Edmund, whose disheveled appearance paired nicely with his expression of discomfort. As Violet turned her back on the Langleys to once again fetch the children, she thought she heard Mrs. Langley say, "Really Edmund, I know we are family, but I cannot have you traipsing around in such a state. Do tidy yourself up a little. A coat and cravat would be a nice start."

Violet smiled to herself slightly. Despite her better judgement, she quite liked Edmund in the state he was in.

Chapter Eight

It had been nearly a fortnight since Edmund had arrived at the Langley estate, and in such a time, he had grown quite a fondness to his niece and nephew's governess. Violet was a pleasant conversationalist, and was sweet in spirit, which was refreshing, when much of Edmund's time was spent with his aloof brother and interdependent sister-in-law. Really, it seemed as though Edmund's time was split between fighting with his brother, or sitting through an insufferably proper afternoon tea or promenade with Katherine. As much as he loved his family, he was beginning to take great joy in escaping them at any chance he got, with the sole object of seeing Violet.

Part of Edmund knew it was wrong, or at least improper, to be so friendly with a member of his brother's staff. He did not wish to put Violet's position at risk were Alfred, or God forbid, Katherine, discover Edmund's slight attachment to their governess. But every time he thought of these reasons to discontinue any familiarity he had her, he thought of more reasons not to.

Violet was much more than his family's governess, was she not? She was her own person, and a beautiful young woman. And though society dictated that she was below Edmund in station, a differing perspective contradicted this. Violet was an educated woman working in a respectable position, as was Edmund an educated man, soon to be working in a respectable position. Really, were they truly that different? And if they were, did it matter?

Edmund's musings were interrupted by his sister-in-law, who appeared in the doorway of the parlor, looking unusually thrilled.

"Edmund, I think you will be pleased that we will have company with dinner tonight." Katherine said this will little exclamation, yet her wide, slim smile shone with more excitement than her tone alluded. Edmund raised his eyebrow, intrigued.

"Really? Anyone I know?" he asked. Katherine scurried across the room and sat in the chair opposite his own. She composed herself as she straightened her skirts and elegantly draped her palms in her lap.

"Yes, indeed," she said. "Ms. Hart is to dine with us. Delightful young lady, is she not?"

Edmund searched his memory for the name Ms. Hart. Ah yes, the one who always giggled and agreed with everything he said. She hadn't given him a particularly agreeable impression in the past, but Edmund could not deny Ms. Hart was very handsome.

"Indeed," Edmund agreed out of politeness.

"Her father was to dine as well, but he is feeling a bit ill, as of late. So we will just be blessed with Ms. Hart's presence."

Edmund only grunted in response; his mind wandered to is brother, as it had been frequently. It was time Edmund did something about his brother's situation, even if only a little.

"Please excuse me, Katherine, I've just remembered I have some business I must attend to." Edmund said, rising from his seat.

"But you will be back in time for dinner, will you not?" Katherine inquired. She rose from her seat as well, so she was eye-level with Edmund.

"I wouldn't miss it," Edmund said with a reassuring smile. He bowed and fled from the room, and for that matter, the Langley estate. Edmund was tired of arguing with his brother and pondering whether he was to help him for not. Edmund had made the decision to help Alfred with his predicament, if only a little, some time ago. Tonight he would give Alfred some money.

*

The evening came swiftly, and with it, the presence of Ms. Isobella Hart. Her soft, handsome features, and golden curls painted her as quite an elegant creature. To dinner Ms. Hart wore a deep blue silk down, which paired nicely with her ocean blue eyes. She was a picture of Venus, some might say.

As Edmund watched her from across the dining room table, he reckoned she was indeed a sight to behold. Yet, Ms. Hart's excessive giggles and flirtations echoed a youth and girlishness, which had not quite left the lady's countenance.

"Dear Ms. Hart has become quite an affectionate companion of mine, Edmund," Katherine said, as the party began their first course of dinner.

"How lovely," Edmund commented, in all politeness. He glanced at his brother, who was sitting at the head of the table, looking quite engrossed in his meal. But at the sound of Ms. Hart's high-pitched giggle, Edmund's gaze drifted back to their dinner guest.

"Mrs. Langley and I have indeed become quite the friends. And her elegance and seasoned knowledge is so educational to learn from." Ms. Hart explained. She smiled sweetly before taking a delicate sip of her wine, holding the glass between her fingertips.

"You are too kind, my dear," cooed Mrs. Langley. She then turned her attention to Edmund. "Ms. Hart is but seventeen years of age, yet she has such promise. She had quite the Season in London last year--and had several marriage proposals!"

"Oh, Mrs. Langley, I am blushing!" cried Ms. Hart, before batting her eyes across the table at Edmund. Now it was his turn to take a sip--a rather large one--of wine.

"Several proposals, and yet you are still unmarried. May I ask why?" Edmund asked. Mrs. Langley looked taken aback at such a bold question, though Ms. Hart seemed rather unfazed.

"Well, I did not love the men who proposed. They were all very wealthy, respectable gentlemen, but I could not see myself marrying a man whom I did not love. I long for someone who earns his own living, and is generous, and kind-hearted. . ."

Ms. Hart let her eyes settle on Edmund with much intensity. Too much, Edmund thought. Was she alluding to someone. . .someone like him? Good God.

Edmund shifted uncomfortably in his seat and looked down at his meal, though he could still feel Ms. Hart's gaze on him. It was to be a long evening, to be sure.

After getting through six courses of food, the ladies exited the dining room, in order to leave the men alone to smoke and drink brandy. Though Edmund was not much of a smoker, and he did not wish to encourage

Alfred to drink, he reveled in the opportunity to have a break from the women.

The two men sat in silence for a time, smoking their cigars, and sipping brandy. The money that Edmund had collected earlier in the day had been burning in his coat pocket for hours now. A part of him was relieved to finally let go of it.

"I have thought a great deal about your... situation." Edmund stated. Alfred took a puff of his cigar.

"Oh?"

"I know we have always had our... issues, with one another. But I wish you to know that I do care about what happens to you and your family," Edmund said. He pulled out a cream envelope from his coat pocket and tossed it to Alfred. His brother swiftly opened it and fingered the envelope's contents, revealing a plentiful stack of crisp banknotes.

"I know it's not nearly enough to fix the situation, but it's the same amount you used to assist me in Oxford."

"Thank you." Alfred said, nodding slightly. His eyes met Edmunds only for a moment, but in such a connection, Edmund saw a warmth in Alfred's icy blue eyes that he had not seen since they were boys. Alfred's gaze quickly steadied back on the money in his hands, yet Edmund knew his brother was grateful to him. The two fell back into silence, but Edmund was content with it. They had an unspoken understanding with one another, and for the first time in a long time, Edmund felt a kinship with his brother.

With much reluctancy, the brothers eventually found their way into the drawing room, where Katherine and Ms. Hart awaited them on the sofa. When Ms. Hart caught sight of Edmund, her countenance perked up quite immensely.

"Gentlemen! Finally you join us! I do so wonder what you men speak of without us in your presence." Ms Hart said. Her blonde curls bounced around her face as she rose from her seat, with Katherine by her side. Edmund glanced at Alfred, whose expression mimicked stone.

"Nothing of interest, I assure you Ms. Hart. We men are boring creatures without our female counterparts." Edmund said. Ms. Hart smiled at such a response, as did Katherine, who had been unusually amiable the entire evening. Edmund did his best to please them, as that was the polite thing to do. However, now that he had come to some form of understanding with his brother for the moment, all Edmund wanted to do was speak with Violet. It was getting late, and he wondered what she was doing. Was she walking in the gardens, among the flowers and newborn stars? Or had she already retired for the night?

"Ms. Hart, will you not play us a song on the pianoforte?" Katherine asked. The comment was enough to draw Edmund from his thoughts of Violet, if only for a moment. Ms. Hart protested, but after Katherine "insisted" on her performance, the young lady practically leapt onto the piano seat, and began sifting through the music sheets. Once her desired song was chosen, Ms. Hart propped the pages upright and fixed her skirts.

"Mr. Langley, would you assist me in turning the music pages while I play?" Ms. Hart asked, looking directly at Edmund, with wide, hopeful eyes. Edmund could do nothing but agree, so he found his way next to Ms. Hart, and waited while she began to play the pianoforte and sing in an unnaturally high tone. It was rather humorous watching Katherine and Alfred from where he stood. Alfred's eyes were narrowed in utter distaste at Ms. Hart's performance, while Katherine beamed with pride, and clapped with much esteem when the girl had finished her song.

Edmund's thoughts had returned back to Violet, which was a subject Edmund's mind seemed to frequent. Tomorrow he would seek her out whenever possible, so he might be in her presence once again. Until then, Edmund would continue his false pleasantries and try to endure the night with a little more decorim than his brother, whose misery in being forced to dine with company was all to apparent on his face. As the night crawled on, Edmund looked out the window to the garden, recalling the night he had walked with Violet at dusk. Something in that memory made him smile.

Until tomorrow, then.

Chapter Nine

Violet could not help but smile as she bathed in the warm hug of the sun. Such beautiful sunny days were not always a guarantee living in England, so when they did, Violet was sure to enjoy it. She sat on the grass, surrounded by the Langley's garden, and breathing in the scent of fresh air and flowers.

Violet had been given an unexpected day off from governess-hood, as Mrs. Langley decided to take the children shopping for ribbons and shoes, without assistance. It was wrong of Violet to judge, but she could not help but wonder whether such a trip with her children was founded solely on motherly love. It seemed Mrs. Langley's interactions with her children relied on her occasional need to prove to her societal acquaintants just how attentive of a mother she was.

Either way, Violet had the entire day to her own, which was something. She basked in her own solitude, not as being lonely, but being peaceful. The song birds sang their soft ballads, while Violet read poetry in the comfort of the sun. Her only shade came from the brim of her bonnet, which was just enough to make reading an easy task.

Violet missed days like this. When her solitude was happy and her thoughts and tribulations were not a constant reminder of things she couldn't have. No Mrs. Langley. No Mr. Langley. No--

"Violet?"

Violet slammed her book shut, startled by the sudden approach of Edmund, who looked immensely handsome in a deep berry-colored coat.

"Mister--Edmund!" Violet exclaimed. She still was not quite used to calling him by his Christain name, yet it gave her an odd pleasure. She quickly scurried to her feet and clawed at her dress, fearing she looked a mess with bits of grass clinging to her skirts. If Edmund noticed, he did not say.

"I did not wish to interrupt your reading," Edmund said, motioning to the book, which Violet still clutched.

"I do not mind." Violet said. It was strange how only moments ago Violet had been utterly content in her solitude, enjoying the quiet company of her own thoughts. Yet, in Edmund's sudden presence, she felt a surge of excitement.

"It appears we are the only ones who have yet to venture off the grounds of the Langley estate," Edmund said. His warm eyes stayed steadfast on Violet's, making her blush.

"Indeed,"

"I was actually just about to walk into town, myself," Edmund said. "To give my letter to the postmaster." He held his folded letter up for Violet to see. The red wax seal shone in the sunlight, reminding Violet of blood.

"I'm sure a servant could send your letter for you." Violet said. A part of her did not wish to see Edmund leave so soon. But Edmund shook his head.

"I prefer to walk myself, and see to my letter's safety. Besides, I was hoping you would accompany me."

"You wish me to walk with you into town? I couldn't!" said Violet.

"I see." Edmund's hopeful expression fell from his face, causing Violet to realize how her words sounded.

"Not that I do not wish to walk with you, because I do," Violet said. Her words were hurried. "But, I fear what some would think to see a governess walking childless and unchaperoned with you."

Edmund nodded slowly and took a step closer to Violet. He smelled of warm masculinity and a clean, freshness, which Violet could not attach to anything besides his person.

"Violet, I am quite certain the strangers in town care not and know not what your or my station is," Edmund said with a confident smile. Violet was utterly aware at how close he was to her--one step closer and they'd be touching. Edmund's close vicinity to her was distracting, but Violet still took in his words. It was true, Violet rarely went into town and thus knew not many of the townspeople there. It was unlikely they would know who she and Edmund were as well...

"Besides, if anyone questions my choice of company, I can tell them you were showing me the way into town, as I have not been around these parts in many years. Which is somewhat true."

"You have truly thought of everything, haven't you?" Violet asked, with a playful giggle.

Edmund gave Violet one of his crooked smiles. "If you must know, I am quite resolute when it comes to getting what I desire."

"Oh? And what is it you desire?"

"I think you know." Edmund said, his voice but a whisper. His expression became serious, as if trying to express an unsaid thought.

Violet swallowed hard, wondering what he could possibly mean. Then, as if realizing his own words, Edmund cleared his throat, and said in a lighter tone, "To walk with you, of course."

"Right," Viold said. She smiled back at Edmund and released her breath. Something told Violet that wasn't what Edmund meant, but she didn't challenge him on it. Instead, she set her book down under a nearby tree, and suggested they better walk swiftly if Edmund wished to catch the postmaster.

The two made their way down the long drive and onto the path into town. For a while, Violet and Edmund were quiet to each other, using the sounds of the wind blowing, and birds chirping, to fill their silences. But these silences were not of discomfort towards one another, Violet reckoned. She was beginning to feel oddly comfortable in Edmund's presence. Though she still felt nervous around him at times, his company gave her a feeling that even her own happy solitude never could.

Violet smiled to herself as she glanced over at Edmund, who was at her side.

"Your letter must be of some importance, the way you grasp it like that." Violet said. Edmund looked down at his hands, which clutched his letter ever so tightly. "You hold it firmly enough to make your fingertips white!" She laughed as she teased him, careful not to allude to Edmund how much she wondered who, in fact, the letter was for.

"Blimey, you're right," Edmund, having realized just how intensely he had been carrying his letter, chuckled. He examined his letter one last time, before tucking it in his coat's inner pocket.

"It's a letter to an old acquaintance of mine back in London. I'm hoping he can assist me with a. . .business matter." Edmund explained as if Violet had indeed asked him what she was wondering.

"And," Violet started. She looked down at her fingers, which she picked as she walked. "Will you be returning to London soon?" She was afraid to hear the answer to this. She could admit to herself that she enjoyed Edmund's company, and feared his departure from the Langley estate.

"Not until I must," Edmund said. His gaze crept to meet Violet's in a sideways glance. "In a few months time I will finish my schooling to become a doctor and take the licensing exam. But until then, I reckon I'll stay here as long as I can."

Violet tried to hide her immense satisfaction by this answer, yet a smile still crept across her face.

"You smile. Does this this please you?"

It did, greatly, but it shouldn't have. She knew in her mind she had no right to enjoy Edmund's company, or even be in his company. It could not end well. Yet, there was nothing more that Violet wanted than to spend the next few months talking with Edmund among the Langley gardens.

"I can say that I find your company pleasant, and thus am pleased to know you will not be leaving the Langley estate for some time."

"I see," Edmund said with a smile. "Well, I'm glad you find my company pleasant. I would have preferred you to greatly esteem my company or for you to be thrilled to know I will not be leaving soon. But I suppose I am pleased that you are pleased."

"Well, I must say I do not greatly esteem your teasing!" Violed said, cheeks skarlett. The two locked eyes and laughed together in a comfort that was now their own.

The two walked on, sharing a constant of smiles and warm looks with one another. Violet was glad no carriages or passerby had found them down the pebbled road, and prayed no one would.

"Surely you miss London and the business of the city?" Violet asked. She was surprised to find Edmund shaking his head.

"London is my home, and I am sure I will miss it at some point. But not at the moment."

The look he gave Violet in that moment sent a shiver down her spine.

Could it be that Edmund had feelings for her? That he found Violet's company more pleasant than he dare say?

No. He couldn't. Could he? Dared she hope? Dared she admit her own growing feelings?

Violet watched as Edmund admired the surrounding trees. His sharp jawline could be very much appreciated from this angle. Appreciated could also be his long eyelashes, which Violet had not known he had possessed until that moment.

Yet it wasn't simply Edmunds looks to which Violet was attracted. And perhaps it wasn't simply attraction. Perhaps it was more than that.

As if panicked at what Violet might discover about herself, she quickly shoved her thoughts down and tucked them away like Edmund's letter. At a later date, perhaps Violet would reevaluate her--feelings--for Edmund. At this place in time, all Violet wanted to do was enjoy her walk with Edmund. And that she did, until they reached town.

Violet distanced herself slightly when she and Edmund reached the heart of town. Shops and homes lined the streets, with men, women and children hustling about, creating a constant buzz of chatter in the air. It was no London, to be sure, but it was the closest Violet would likely ever get to it.

Edmund quickly deposited his letter to the postmaster, ensuring its safe delivery, while Violet kept her wide eyes searching for any face she might have known. Her eyes grazed over an older woman, then two men walking past, and a girl with bright red hair. None were familiar, and thus would not pose a threat to Violet and Edmund. She took a deep breath and slowly let it out as Edmund approached.

"Shall we head back?" Violet asked.

"Yes, let's," Edmund replied, scanning his environment one last time. He squinted his eyes as the sunlight attacked his vision, and drifted his gaze past Violet. Instead of leaving with Violet, Edmund suddenly stiffened, and his countenance became rigid and alert.

What did he see? Violet's heartbeat quickened in utter fear of what Edmund saw behind her. Was it Mrs. Langley, prepared to scold them with her seemingly natural look of disapproval? Or that maid Mary? She would likely leap at the chance to cause trouble if she saw Violet out with Edmund.

Violet's stomach twisted this way and that, like a wet rag being rung out. Slowly, she turned her head and followed the direction of Edmund's fixed stare. To her surprise, she saw no one she knew. People continued to stroll down the road, as shops hustled with business. It seemed everyone was quite ignorant of Violet and Edmund's presence.

"What is it?" Violet asked. Edmund's gaze did not waver back to Violet. Instead he began walking past her, as if deaf to her questioning, until he approached the town's public house. Violet followed from behind. She reckoned it was rather early in the day to be dwelling in the pub, yet several horses were tied out front, waiting for their masters to return to them.

Edmund approached a large black horse, which looked vaguely familiar to Violet. The massive beast flickered his tail at their approach, yet stayed quiet. Edmund clenched his jaw as his fingers grazed the white star marking on the horse's nose.

"This is my brother's horse," Edmund finally said. Violet knew not what to say. She wondered why Edmund seemed so displeased. It was no secret that Alfred Langley was rather fond of drink, and likely spent much time at the public house.

A sudden wave of men laughing drifted outside.

"If you do not mind, will you wait for me while I go inside for a moment?"

Violet's confused expression seemed to answer before her words could. So Edmund elaborated. "Not to get a drink--I-I want to. . . speak with my brother for a moment and check in with him." Edmund's sudden serious expression mixed with that of, worry, was it? It unsettled Violet to be sure.

"No, of course I do not mind," she said. "Go in, I will wait." Edmund gave her a quick nod of thanks before disappearing into the building.

She stood among the horses, feeling unsure of what to do with herself, and wondering what Edmund was doing inside. It felt as though Violet had been waiting outside for a fortnight, but it could have only been a few minutes. And it was a few minutes more before the sound of men shouting at one another ripped through the building and hit Violet's ears like a crack of lightning. Her heart quickened its pace again as she strained to make out what was being said.

What was happening inside? Was Edmund alright?

Violet could not make out what was being said, as layer upon layer, men's voices began to shout at one another. In a flash, she thought back to the day she found the Langley brothers arguing, and recalled how heated both men had seemed. What if the brothers were fighting again and it escalated? Anything could happen in a place such as this. Something had to be done.

With Edmund on Violet's mind and not much else, she slipped into the pub. It was darker inside than she had expected, and she had to cover her nose from the overwhelming stench of alcohol and male musk. She quickly regretted her entrance, but as she slipped through the crowd of men and pretended not to notice their stares on her, she knew she could not turn back. Raised voices became louder as she approached the back of the room.

"Once again Alfred, you seem to ruin yourself with much success. Apparently it is the only thing you are good for!"

Edmund's voice rose above the other shouts, causing Violet to catch her breath. A small room sat off to the left of the main pub room, where Violet suspected the Langley brothers were. She stopped at the doorway to the room, not daring to enter. Instead, she planted herself just right, so she could watch the commotion from outside the room.

Alfred sat at a small table surrounded by men and playing cards, while clutching his essential accessory--a glass of brandy. Edmund, who was looking quite red in the face, towered above him in a fury.

"Oh bugger off Edmund," Alfred barked. He slammed his drink down on the table, spilling drops of brown liquid on the playing cards.

"I simply cannot understand why you would gamble away the money I gave you, when gambling is the very act which got you in your current situation!"

Violet's mouth fell open in shock. She actually had to lift her hand to her chin in order to close her parted lips. Once again she somehow found herself eavesdropping on a situation which should be kept private. What had she been thinking to burst into the pub--as if she could do anything to stop the Langley brothers from fighting. If anything, Violet would make things worse. But her curiosity had gotten to her, and had, at this point, almost completely paralyzed her.

"You and I both knew that my debts are bigger than a few thousand pounds. I had no other option but to seek a more sizable amount of money."

"There are always other options, Alfred."

"So you keep telling me! But what other options do you suggest? How do you suggest I attain enough money to cover my debts before the man I am indebted to claims my livelihood?"

Men holared around them, taking sides between the brothers and spitting unwholesome remarks at the prospect of violence. Edmund furrowed his brows.

"Your livelihood?"

Alfred Langley clenched his jaw in discomfort as he hunched over the table. The dim lighting in the room shadowed his eyes, hollowing his face like a ghost in a gothic novel. When he spoke again, his voice was lowered. Violet, still clung to the beam of the doorway, strained to make out the elder Mr. Langey's next words.

"My debt is even greater than I let on. If I don't pay them soon, I will lose the estate."

Violet gasped.

"Bloody hell," Edmund muttered.

The Langey's were in debt? But they appeared so wealthy and comfortable in their living. Violet never would have guessed that it was possible that someone like Alfred Langley, a man born into wealth and status, could struggle to keep his steady living.

Flashes of Edmund shouting at his brother appeared in Violet's head. "Apparently it is only my money that you need." That is what Edmund had said, wasn't it? And when Violet and Edmund walked in the garden together some evenings ago--Edmund had been trying to make an important decision of some kind. Was that decision to lend his brother money?

Violet was slowly piecing together the possible events which lead up to this moment between brothers. The Langeys were in debt. They could lose everything.

Violet was pulled out of her thoughts when Alfred Langley rose from his seat and leered at the other men in the room, as if seeing them for the first time. A suffocating silence fell upon the room.

"What the hell are you looking at?" he barked. A man coughed in the distance, but no response came to Mr. Langley. He turned to his younger brother.

"If it makes a difference, I won four-hundred pounds."

"But how much did you lose in the process?"

Edmund turned towards the doorway to leave. Violet, still frozen by the shock of the past events, could not move fast enough.

They locked eyes.

By the grace of God, she found her footing and turned on her heal. Violet flitted back through the front of the public house, bumping into strange men and spitting apologies along the way. Finally, Violet pushed open the front door and panted in the fresh of the sun.

He hadn't seen her, had he?

Edmund appeared outside within a few seconds, surprise still in those mahogany eyes of his.

"Violet," Edmund started.

Violet bit her lip. He had seen her. He knew she had been eavesdropping on his conversation. Again.

"I do apologize. I didn't mean--I shouldn't have--again." Her words came out in pieces that did not quite fit together. She was so embarrassed. What Edmund must have thought of her! Would he be angry with her?

But to Violet's surprise, when Edmund approached her, there was no anger left inside of him. It seemed all of that emotion had been drained by his brother. Instead, before Violet, stood a man who looked defeated and rather tired.

"I don't know what to do," Edmund said softly. "I can only help him so much."

Violet nodded. She watched him slumber towards her, rubbing his eyes in the process.

"Come, let us leave." said Violet. So they did.

The two made their way back down the road, and on to the pathway leading to the Langley residence. Soon they were alone, and left in their own silences. Violet did not dare to speak, as she knew not what to say. She kept opening her mouth to say something of consolation to Edmund, but no combination of words seemed quite right. So instead, Edmund was the one who decided to speak. He kept his eyes focused on the road ahead, but his words were meant for Violet. He told her about his argument with his brother, when he discovered the Alfred was in debt.

"I knew it was a sizable amount, but I had no idea--no none whatsoever, that it was enough for him to lose the estate," he said.

"Does Mrs. Langley know?"

Edmund shook his head. He then told her about how his brother stole Mrs. Langley's jewelry, and let her lady's maid take the blame. And about how Edmund had given him money to help pay his debts, but Alfred had just gambled it away.

Violet stayed quiet and let him release everything to her. As they walked and she listened to him, Edmund's countenance slowly began to soften. It was almost as though he was relieved to tell Violet these things. By the time they made their way back to the Langley estate, Edmund was nearly out of breath from speaking so much.

"The letter I sent today was actually to a boy I used to go to boarding school with. Well, I suppose he's no longer a boy. Anyway, he's a lawyer now, and thought he might be able to help the situation, but now, now I don't know." Edmund said.

Violet and Edmund seemed to somehow find their way back into the gardens, staring at the massive home from afar. It stood several stories tall, each level dotted with glass windows. It would be quite something to lose such a place.

"Perhaps I would wash my hands of the entire ordeal and head back to London early."

"Don't do that," Violet said, a little too panicked. She blushed and tried again. "You can only do so much, Edmund. But at least you'll know you've tried to help. If not for Mr. Langley, but for Mrs. Langley and little Charlotte and Fredric. You're not responsible for what your brother has done. But the least you can do is support the rest of your family through such trialling times, even if they do not know what is to come."

Edmund sighed and ran his fingers through his hair.

"You're right," he said. "I am glad you know about this all now. I was in dire need of someone to vent this too." He gave Violet a gentle smile.

"Know that you have my utmost discretion, Edmund."

"I know."

They stood together there for a while, studying the sharp edges of Langley House, and how it cast shade over the large stone steps leading up to the front door. She found comfort in his closeness in that moment. His coated arm indeed kept grazing her own bare arm. It tickled her skin and made her smile. And thought that was an amiable distraction, it was not enough to push a certain thought aside which had kept coming back to her: If the Lanleys were in debt and lose their estate, than surely Violet would be out of a job, wouldn't she?

Chapter Ten

"Lord. Alby." Alfred huffed, struggling for breath. He lunged at Edmund, thrusting his foil sword at him. Edmund parried his brother's attack, blocking the blade from any contact with his skin.

Lord Alby. So this was the man who held Alfred's livelihood by its throat. Edmund knew not the man, but as his title suggested, he was a member of the nobility.

Edmund counterattacked with a riposte, which was blocked by Alfred. Their swords clashed together, the satisfying clink of metal bringing Edmund from his thoughts.

"And how did you meet this--Lord Alby?"

Edmund now lunged at his brother, sword and arm extended outwards. Alfred leaned back, just missing the tip of Edmund's blade.

"At the. Gentleman's club," Alfred breathed heavily, but managed to jab his foil at Edmund, grazing him at his ribs. The men immediately lowered their weaponry, and backed away from each other, resetting their dueling positions.

"Ah, so your gambling adventures do not end at the public house. How am I not surprised?" Edmund scoffed, not nearly as devoid of breath as Alfred.

"Gambling is a. Gentleman's past time, Edmund. Do not act as though. You are above it."

Edmund opened his mouth to reply, but thought better of it. Nothing he could say to Alfred would take away his brother's debts. Sarcasm and judgmental comments would be given in vain. Instead, Edmund clenched his jaw and lunged at his brother with his sword.

Fencing was the one sport in which both Langley men enjoyed, though they rarely dueled together. When Edmund was a young boy, he remembered watching his older brother fence with much skill. Such power and precision, each move more calculated than the last. Fencing made Alfred seem of some authority, and someone to look up to. At the time, Edmund was much too young to learn the sport himself, but when he went off to boarding school, and years passed, Edmund found the same power and precision in fencing that Alfred had had.

The brothers continued to yield their swords at one another, in a rhythmic pattern of lunge, parrie, riposte; lunge, parrie, riposte.

"I have a fortnight. To pay Lord Alby. Before he claims. My estate."

Edmund, about to lunge at Alfred, lowered his sword.

"A fortnight? That is not nearly enough time to collect such a large sum of money."

"I know. But there is nothing to do about it."

Alfred grabbed the hem of his shirt and brought it to his face, wiping away the stinging droplets of sweat. The light of the sun shone on Alfred, revealing large damp spots on his untucked shirt, and silver scruff collecting on his face. Edmund realized his brother wasn't as young and powerful as he once used to be. It was the end of many things, Edmund reckoned. It was... disappointing, to be sure.

"Have you no fight left in you?" Edmund asked suddenly. The meaning of his words bled through the context of fencing, like a wound bleeding through bandages.

Catching Edmund's words, Alfred promptly threw them back at him.

"Have I no fight left?" My entire life I've been fighting!"

"Yet you give up so easily," Edmund said. He knew it was wrong of him to say this, and that he shouldn't. But he did. How easy it was to provoke his brother, and how quickly his brother would counterattack.

"Perhaps if you had had my life, you would not judge me for my own follies. You have no idea what it was like living with Father. I had to defend and I had to fight every day until he died, while you were shipped away to become educated."

"Because that was my choice," Edmund cut in, the sarcasm he had pledged to hold back now released.

"I had to endure hell with him, Edmund! You have no idea."

"You're right, I don't. I barely remember anything about our father. But what I do know, is that you've turned out just like him."

Edmund's words pierced Alfred with more force than a sword ever could. He regretted saying it immediately, but there was truth to his statement. Alfred had turned into the same violent, drunkard, who seemed to rely on anyone but his own self. Still, Edmund felt his own vice in his words. His mind drifted suddenly to Violet, and with much surprise, he found himself wondering what she would think of his words to Alfred. She had advised him to support his family through these trying times, though here he was, fighting with his brother yet again. It was strange to admit that Edmund cared about what Violet thought of him, but he did.

"Alfred, I didn't mean that," Edmund said, his voice softer now. Alfred said nothing, but his eyes were hardened icicles. Why did they always do this?

Worless, Alfred crept closer to Edmund, his jaw tightening. Edmund was quite certain his brother was about to attack him. Alfred lifted his sword and held the tip against Edmund's heart. It did not hurt him, as the foil sword was only for practice, and thus blunted. Still, the motion felt like an attack on Alfred's part, igniting another flicker of fiery in Edmund's gut.

"What are you to do to me, Alfred? Attack me with a blunted weapon?" he asked. Edmund dropped his own foil sword, letting it fumble at his feet. "Perhaps your anger with me would be better suited by your fists. Is that not how father handled his anger?"

Yes, Violet would most definitely disapprove of Edmund's actions. But Violet was nowhere in sight at the moment, was she?

Within a blink, Alfred threw his sword side and lunged at Edmund. This time, it wasn't for fencing, and the contact that Alfred's fist made with Edmund's face, was indeed, not for practice. Edmund, in return, grabbed his brother by the collar, and pushed him away. His forearms tensed as he struggled with Alfred. He could tell from the sting of his eye that it would soon swell and blacken.

The two men wrestled with each other for a time, in a brotherly quarrel.

"Gentlemen," a familiar voice called in the distance. "Ehem!"

Edmund vaguely recognized the shrill call of Katherine Langley. However, he and Alfred continued to grip each others' arms in a back-and-forth struggle.

"Gentlemen!" Katherine shouted. Her voice nearly echoed over the trees. It was enough to break the brothers apart. They released each other, each giving the other one last forceful push as they broke apart. Katherine stood between them, eyes narrowed. Her lips were pressed together in a thin line of disapproval.

"What is the meaning of this?" Katherine shrieked. The brothers glanced at each other and before one of them could speak, Katherine held up her hand to stop them. "No, nevermind. I do not care. What I care about is that you both put your quarrel behind you, as Ms. Hart will be calling on us."

Edmund and Alfred stood, out of breath and red cheeked, like children who were being reprimanded by their mother. They stood in silence, neither of them wishing to speak.

"I expect that you both clean up and fulfill your duty of behaving like respectable men."

Edmund and Alfred shared a small glance, and nodded slightly. It was as close they'd get to apologizing to each other. Katherine raised her eyebrows expectantly.

"Now!" she commanded. Edmund sighed and rubbed his sore face as he strolled back to the house. It was going to take a lot of effort to prepare for Ms. Hart's company. She had been calling on them quite frequently, and each visitation became more difficult for Edmund to bare. Ms. Hart was a lovely lady, but she could be rather insufferable.

*

Sunday came, and with it, a promenade to church. Since Edmund and Violet's walk to town, they had not spoken to one another. Ms. Hart seemed to be at the Langley estate almost every day, and as such, she had taken much of Edmund's attention. She had never felt a strong like or dislike of Ms. Hart before, but Violet was quickly beginning to resent the young lady's presence. Just the other day, Violet had glanced out the window from the school room, while the children were practicing their letters. To her surprise, she found Edmund and Ms. Hart, strolling about the gardens. Ms. Hart's dainty arm rested on Edmund's, as they walked together. She looked so beautiful and elegant draped at his side, her silk dress flowing down her slim figure like a waterfall. She laughed and smiled at him, causing Violet's stomach to feel weighted, and her throat to feel bloated.

What was this feeling that Violet so violently felt? Could it be jealousy?

And now, as Violet walked to church with the Langley party, with the inclusion of Ms. Hart of course, the same feelings flooded Violet's veins. Mr. and Mrs. Langley lead the group down the pebbled road. Large ostrich feathers waved in the wind like a flag, which were promptly attached to Mrs. Langley's bonnet. Ms. Hart walked behind them with Edmund. She clung to him with such an open familiarity it made Violet's face burn. She thought back to her walk to town with Edmund, and how she flirted with the notion that Edmund had become attached, in some way, to Violet. But as she watched him walking with Ms. Hart, she felt like a fool.

Violet was sure she was nothing like the elegant ladies of London, or even like Ms. Hart. Why would he fancy Violet when he had an endless array of wealthy, sophisticated women to choose from? Violet felt silly for even entertaining the thought in her mind. Edmund was friendly with Violet because he enjoyed her company, he said it himself. Surely enjoying her company did not mean Edmund fancied her. What a silly, though fleeting notion that had been. The waves of disappointment and jealousy which wet her heart, were best left uninvestigated, Violet reckoned. Even defining these emotions was dangerously close to defining any feelings she had toward Edmund.

Not that she had any.

Violet's grip tightened on Charlotte and Fredric, who each filled a hand. She walked with the children some feet behind Edmund and Ms. Hart, trying to ignore Ms. Hart's girlish giggles.

That morning's sermon was difficult to focus on. Instead, Violet found her attentions on the back of Edmund's neck and Ms. Hart's bonnet, the latter which came dangerously close to grazing the former, on multiple occasions. Ms. Hart seemed to take every opportunity to lean into Edmund, especially when they shared a hymn book during times of song. As they sung the hymns, which Violet knew by heart, she watched Ms. Hart give Edmund secret glances every other verse. The young lady was somehow able to smile gaily whilst in mid-song, in much flirtation. How shameless, Ms. Hart was. And in church!

But then, the service ended, and the Langley party began shuffling out of church. Mrs. Langley, the conversationalist that she was, quickly found acquaintances to speak to once outside. Violet stood off to the side, watching the children play in the church's graveyard. They darted around the stone graves like little mice. As she watched, Violet began playing with her fingered, twisting them this way and that, in an uncomfortable wait for her party. It was during this minor activity, in which she realised there was in fact nothing in her hands. Violet's bible was missing.

"Oh, my..." she started, but didn't bother finishing her exclamation, as no one was listening. Just as she was about to go back inside in search of her Bible, Edmund appeared with the leather-bound book in hand. He handed it to her, his eyes hidden by the shadows of the brim of his top hat.

"My Bible! Thank you, Mr. Langley," Violet said.

"My pleasure," he said. He smiled softly, before rejoining Ms. Hart's side. Violet's heart sank at her fleeting interaction with him. But as she looked down at her Bible, she noticed a small piece of paper sticking out from between two of the pages.

What was this?

Violet furrowed her brows and opened the black book carefully. A thick, creamy piece of paper had been carefully placed inside. It stood out considerably compared to the thin, delicate pages of the Bible. Still, the folded paper would seem hidden to anyone but the book's owner. Violet slowly unfolded the note and read its brief contents.

Violet, meet me in the garden maze at dusk. -E.L.

E.L. Edmund Langley.

A surge of hope flooded Violet's heart. Edmund wish to see her? But what did that mean? Violet knew not how to feel, but her stomach was indeed in agony.

It seemed as though the rest of the day took an increasingly long time to make its end. Each minute dragged on longer than the next, shamelessly making Violet wait for dusk, distressed and in wonder of what would happen.

But finally, the sun began to fall, causing the sky to take on its fiery colors. The air was cooler outside, and as Violet skirried to the beginning of the hedge maze, she reveled in the drowsy quietness. She paced back and forth between the hedge walls, waiting for Edmund's presence.

"Violet!"

Violet's pacing habits stopped short when she heard Edmund call her name in a deep whisper. He appeared at the entrance to the hedge, but stepped no farther inside.

"You found my note," he said with a gentle smile.

"Hello Edmund," Violet whispered. Her heart was a little guarded, after seeing him so close with Ms. Hart. She would not allow herself become affected in any way by Edmund. No, not anymore.

Violet was much more affected by movement in the distance. She looked past Edmond, and, to her dismay, spotted a figure walking near. Violet tensed, and her eyes widened in panic.

"What is the matter?"

Violet found herself unable to answer Edmund's question. Her heart throbbed with the fear that she and Edmund would be caught together. The folly of fear is that it often leads to action without ration, as it slowly suffocates the fearful. Violet found this to be true that evening. Before she knew what she was doing, she had grabbed Edmund's arms and pulled him forward, into the hedge maze. Violet's only thought was to get him out of sight, and into the safety of the hedges. Yet by doing so, he had stumbled forward and pressed into her, so close that their noses nearly touched. How quick Violet was to realize how tight a grip she held on Edmund's strong arms, which were still awkwardly extended from her tug. Edmund said nothing past his initial surprised expression. His eyes flickered from Violet's eyes to her mouth, which was scandalously too close to his own.

"I saw someone coming," Violet said softly, in an attempt to explain her impropriety.

"Likely the stableboy," Edmund muttered. His eyes seemed utterly distracted by Violet's lips. So much so, that Violet thought it best to release her hold on him, and birth a separation between their two figures. She bowed her head and twisted her fingers, trying not to blush. Apparently her efforts were in vain to resist affectation from Edmund. She bit her lip.

"Well then, shall we take a stroll about the hedges?" Edmund asked. Violet looked up at him and nodded. As he approached her side, the setting sun hit his face, revealing for the first time, a swollen and bruised left eye. She gasped in shock at the sight, and the caregiver that she was, instinctively raised her hand to assess the damage. Though, as God was on her side, Violet quickly thought better of it, and lowered her hand.

"Your eye!" Violet exclaimed instead. At the mention of his eye, Edmund raised his own hand to the damaged body part.

"Ah, yes, my eye," he said. He bowed his head and stiffened, as if uncomfortable with the mention of his wound. Had he gotten in a brawl? If he had, with whom? Likely his brother, Violet guessed. And she was right. Edmund, though apprehensive, told her as much.

"Alfred and I. . . we had a bit of a disagreement. . . that is all."

"Oh," Violet said. "About his. . .situation?"

"Yes, something like that," said Edmund. He did not elaborate on the subject, and Violet reckoned it was not her place to pry. Instead, they slowly walked together, making somewhat familiar turns throughout the maze, even in the dimmed light. The nearby trees brought in a soft summer breeze, which kissed Violet's skin, giving her a refreshing shiver.

Violet and Edmund walked together for a few moments in the softness of the garden. Being reminded of the Langley's debt brought forth Violet's recurring fear that she would soon be out of a job.

As if reading her mind, Edmund asked suddenly, "What are you thinking of, at this moment?"

"At this moment?"

Edmund watched Violet, as she thought about his question. His eyes, even though damaged, managed to study her softly, as if he was able to see through to her soul. Such a look would have caused much vexation to

Violet, perhaps even just a fortnight ago. Yet, she was somehow comforted by Edmund's stare.

"I--well, I was thinking of what might happen to me, and the security of my position, should, your brother. . . succumb to his debts," Violet started. Before Edmund could reply, she quickly added, "I know it is selfish of me to think of, but it has crossed my mind that Ms. Langley's--misfortunes--might translate into my own."

Violet feared what Edmund thought of her from such a statement, but she was only telling the truth. She could not pretend that she was in a standing where work was not part of her livelihood. She was not a lady like Ms. Hart, who likely relied on a large inheritance and prospective husbands to live comfortably. Violet had to work for a place to live, food to eat, and for money to give to her mother. Her position as a governess was her life, and indeed vital to every part of her being. Violet argued such statements in her own mind, as if trying to convince herself that her concerns were valid.

"I don't think it selfish at all," Edmund said. His expression was soft and his tone lacked any kind of judgement. "Though quite frankly, I believe your position as governess to be most secure."

Violet's furrowed brow and tilted head asked for an explanation to his words. Edmund elaborated.

"What I mean is, Katherine, er, Mrs. langley, well, she would not be willing to give up a governess for her children, no matter her financial situation. Not having you in her household would be devastating to her social standing."

"That is comforting, I suppose," Violet said. She questioned the legitimacy of Edmund's statement, but she trusted he knew his own sister in-law.

"But, if you were to lose your position, know that I wouldn't let you fend for yourself," Edmund said. His tone was serious, but then he smiled. "Perhaps I could hire you as my own governess."

"And what would I teach you?" Violet asked, beginning to chuckle. Edmund have her a mischievous shrug. "I'm sure there are many things you could teach me. Or, if you'd prefer, I could find some children to keep? Perhaps the Browns' have a few to spare."

Violet, inelegant as it was, snorted with laughter. The Browns were a family which Mrs. Langley spoke of often, as she found much delight in keeping competition with them.

Violet found Edmund had a way of comforting her in a way that distracted her from her own worries, until they were both sharing laughs and smiles. It was a talent no other person had ever had with her. The two, having been faced with a large wall of greenery, turned on their heels and traveled down another pathway of hedges.

"Pray tell, why did you ask to see me this evening?" Violet asked boldly. Her growing comfort with Edmund was giving her more courage to ask him questions in her mind. Her heart fluttered as it waited for a response. Edmund furrowed his brows, creating little folds on his forehead.

"Need I a particular reason? Other than simply wishing to be in your company?"

His response made Violet blush.

"No, I suppose not," she said.

*

That night, Violet struggled not to smile as she readied herself for bed. She sat upright in her narrow bed, brushing her long chocolate hair in a daze.

Every time Violet was with Edmund, another piece of her was changed in some way. Whether she liked it or not, her heart cherished any time spent with him. Even if his affections truly belonged to Ms. Hart, Violet could no longer deny that her own affections belonged to Edmund. Her better judgement and rational thought had long ago been overpowered by a feeling that Violet had never felt before. She still wasn't quite sure what it was, but it prevented her from caring that her heart tugged her to a future that could never be. To a person that could never be hers.

But it didn't matter, not at the moment.

Violet glanced at her small bedside table, atop which sat her bible. The memory of Edmund's note clung to her, causing her to fling her brush onto her bed and retrieve the note from the holy book. Edmund enjoyed hiding things in books, didn't he?

Violet brushed her fingertips across Edmund's handwriting. His letters were small in stature, but she could tell they had been written with an aggression which only a man could naturally express through ink. He pressed down too hard on the paper as he wrote, yet his education had at least ensured a neatness to his handwriting, not often found in his sex.

Violet smiled to herself. She ought to burn the little note, as it was evidence that Violet and Edmund were connected in some way. She glanced at the well-used candle, which burned at her bedside. It would be foolish not to burn it, for the purpose of a keepsake. Yet, Violet had given away the honeysuckle that Edmund had sent her. This little note, Edmund's little words--they were the only physical thing she had which tied to Edmund. Should she not allow herself this one foolish pleasure?

Before Violet could change her mind, she blew out the candle, breathing in the comforting smoke as the room absorbed the darkness. She gently placed the paper note under her pillow, and laid her head down. It was an odd comfort, knowing it was under her pillow. She only hoped she wouldn't regret keeping it.

Chapter Eleven

"Ay me, for aught that I could ever read, could ever hear by tale or history--

"The course of true love never did run smooth."

Violet looked up from her book in surprise, not intending for another voice to complete the quote. She had been reading A Midsummer Night's Dream to the children for some weeks now, yet little Charlotte and Fredric were too young to quote Shakespeare.

But of course, there he was, Edmund, standing in the doorway with a quiet smile on his face.

"Edmund," Violet said. "I did not know your were so well acquainted with Shakespeare." At the sound of his uncle's name, Fredric jumped to his feet and tackled Edmund with his tiny arms. Of course, at the fesh age of four, Freddy was still quite short, and thus he only managed to embrace his uncle's legs.

"I know a little of Shakespeare, let us not use the term 'well acquainted'." Edmund said with a chuckle. He scooped up Fredric in his arms and carried him over his shoulder to where Violet and Charlotte were sitting on the sofa. The way Edmund was looking down on Violet made her heart smile brightly. She opened her mouth to speak to him, but pressed her lips back together when Mrs. Langley and Ms. Hart appeared behind Edmund.

"We are reading in the drawing room today!" Charlotte said cheerfully to her mother, whose expression was that of surprise when she entered the room.

"I see," Mrs. Langley said, lacking any warmth in her words. Ms. Hart drifted to where Edmund stood with Freddy still in his arms.

"What an adorable child!" Ms. Hart cried, rubbing her finger against Freddy's plump cheeks. Violet, on the other hand, rose from her seat and straightened, heart pounding. Why did she fear Mrs. Langley so? Was it her constant vexed and judgemental dimenor? Or was it the ever looming threat of her authority to throw Violet out on the streets whenever she wished?

"And Miss Violet, why is it that you are reading here, in the drawing room?" Mrs. Langley asked. Her inquiry was innocent enough, yet her demeanor proved to be less than thrilled by Violet's presence. Violet, who had slipped into her nervous chattering, tried to quickly explain.

"Well, you see, the ceiling to the school room appears to be leaking--it is raining quite vigorously today. I placed a vase underneath the leak to collect the water, but I reckoned the conditions of the room were too poor to teach the children in," she explained.

"I see."

"It was also quite drafty."

Mrs. Langley, elegant as ever, carefully draped her tall figure on a nearby chair. Her hardened eyes were clearly unimpressed by Violet's excuses, yet she said nothing. Nobody said anything, as a matter of fact. All that could be heard was the pouring rain outside the window, pounding the ground with a beautiful violence, which only nature was capable of. Violet felt the pressure of her companions' silence pressing upon her chest, clearly feeling unwanted in the room. But just as she was about to suggest her leave with the children, Edmund said the most surprising of things.

"I believe a happy birthday is in order, Miss Violet."

"It is your birthday?" Ms. Hart asked. Her blonde ringlets bounced about her face at the inquiry.

"Yes," Violet said to Ms. Hart. Her eyes then wandered back to Edmund's. "How ever did you know?"

"Fredric might have mentioned it to me yesterday. You must be careful what you tell these children, as they share any bit of information given with the utmost ease." Edmund said with a foolish grin. Violet smiled at him, but when their gaze was caught by Ms. Hart, her eyes darted to the floor.

"Well, isn't that lovely. You know, I have heard the Brown's used to invite their governess to dine with them on special occasions, such as a birthday." Ms. Hart said cheerfully.

"Really?" Mrs. Langley raised an eyebrow. "How intimate of them." Scepticism dripped from her words, causing Violet to hold back chuckles. She knew Mrs. Langley was in constant competition with the Brown family. The lady made it her duty to do everything they were doing and then some, so she might prove to be superior, in some way, to them.

"Isn't that splendidly kind of them? Mrs. Brown says she is in utter dismay now that their governess has left them. She is gone, and little Daniel Brown is off to boarding school, and Mrs. Brown says the house feels so lonely. Apparently she quite liked Daniel's governess--she was very liked indeed, by the whole family. "

"Is that so?" Mrs. Langley asked. The lady's upper lip had stiffened greatly since the beginning of Ms. Hart's innocent speech on the Brown's. It was quite comical to watch, as Ms. Hart clearly had no awareness of Mrs. Langley's true thoughts. Unfortunately, the comical nature of the situation disappeared almost immediately, when Mrs. Langley invited Violet to dinner.

"Well then, Miss Violet, would you not join us for dinner tonight, in honor of your birthday?" The words were forced out of her, as if they were painful to ask. Violet's smile, which she had been suppressing with Edmund, disappeared. Surely her face had turned red as well, as the panic set in. Dinner with the Langey's? How horrifyingly uncomfortable that would be! Mr. Langley would grunt in disgust at any effort made at pleasantries, and would likely ban any laughter at the dinner table. Mrs. Langley would surely interrogate Violet, and be unimpressed with any attempts Violet would make at answering her. It would be uncomfortable, and so, so--

"What a splendid idea," Edmund said.

Well, perhaps the dinner wouldn't be completely awful, with Edmund present. Still, Violet thought it best to protest, if not a little.

"Really, that is very kind of you, but there is no need to do anything for my birthday--truly."

"I'll hear none of that. I insist that you have dinner with us. And Ms. Hart, won't you join us for dinner as well?"

"I would love to!" Ms. Hart said, smiling brightly.

"Then it is settled," Mrs. Langley said, with finality. "Now, Miss Violet, I give you leave of the children for the day to prepare yourself for dinner."

"That is very kind of you, but--

"I reckon you'll need plenty of time to make yourself presentable. I should hope you own anything other than an apron?"

Violet bit her lip, trying desperately not to react to Mrs. Langley's back-handed insult.

"I'm sure I can find something presentable." Violet said with a forced smile. Making no haste, she swiftly excused herself and made her way to her bed chamber, so she might prep herself for the eventful evening. She was still quite stressed over dining with the Langey's, yet a bit of her was excited. It was not often she was able to dress nicely. It did not take long for her to pull out her only suitable dress, which had not ever been worn.

Violet curressed the fine muslin fabric, which had been much too expensive for her family to afford, even when her father was living. Yet, there the beautiful fabric had been, carefully packaged in brown paper and positioned on the dining table for her four years ago. Violet had been but seventeen then. Her Papa had insisted on having a proper seamstress tailor a dress for her, using the fine fabric. It was extravagantly made to the latest fashion--a grecian empire waistline with short puffed sleeves. It was simple but elegant.

Violet held the frock up to her frame, which draped narrowly down her body. The dress had been meant for her coming of age. She was to come out into society and have her first season in London. Violet had been thrilled at the prospect, yet she remembered protesting to her father.

"I am grateful, Papa, but I am not blind to our circumstances. You have always given me a comfortable living, but a season in London? However will it be afforded?"

"Fret not my dear. These matters are not for your concern." Papa had said. He had rubbed the top of her hand with his thumb, a regular consolation tactic of his. Violet missed those those gentle, reassuring touches from him.

"I am but a--

"Do not say that you are but a clergyman's daughter. You are more than that. I am more than a clergyman," Papa had said. "We give ourselves titles and depend on them to define us. To separate us from one another. But you are no less worthy of that frock or a season in London than any other young lady. We are all God's children, after all."

Violet could never argue with her father for long. She could not protest his convictions and speeches. He had a way about him which could not be contended. So Violet had agreed to it all--the beautiful dress, the coming out, the season in London. She was ready to begin her life as a lady, and with any luck, a wife. Something she had always quietly dreamt about. But she had never worn the dress, nor had she gone to London. Her father had died before it could be done, and everything changed.

Now Violet stood in front of her lookingglass, clutching the memory of her father in her hands. So very much had changed since that day, hadn't it?

Violet carefully slipped off the worn grey dress she wore and tossed it on her bed. She untied her hair and let her dark locks fall about her, mustering the courage to put on the frock. It was the color of dark violet.

"Violet for my Violet." Papa had said. As she dressed in the evening gown, Violet thought how glad she was she had never given the dress away. After her father's death, Violet was looking for work, and she and her mother had struggled greatly to live comfortably again. Violet had considered trying to sell the beautiful dress, but thus, could not. Part of it was that the dress gave her a small memory her father. However, perhaps a part of her also hoped if she kept the frock long enough, her ownership of it would not be in vain. That one day, she would have a reason so wear such a fine dress.

That day had come.

As Violet walked down the hall to dinner, she noticed the servants she passed began to stare. The male servants widened their eyes and looked at her with a gobsmacked expressions. The female servants narrowed their eyes as they watched her pass by, likely wondering why the governess was dressed like a lady of the house, rather than as the servant that she was. Their stares made Violet conscious of her looks. The frock's square neckline cut slightly lower than what she was used to, which was enough to give her anxieties. She hoped she did not look a fool all dressed up, pretending, just for one night, that she was not a servant.

Violet met the Langleys and Ms. Hart in the parlor. When she entered, the room's chatter all fell silent, even Mrs. Langley. Eyes once again fell on Violet, for some horrifying reason. Did she look as though she had tried too hard? Her hair was pinned up with intricate plaits, and delicate ringlets encircled her face, as she had seen many gentile women style their hair. Of course it was no match for Ms. Hart's golden locks, which were pinned up with an intricate scattering of pearls upon her head.

"Good evening," Violet managed to say. Edmund sprung from his chair with an excess of enthusiasm.

"Miss Violet!" Edmund said. He seemed to be fighting off a grin at the sight of her. His excitement did not go unnoticed, namely by Ms. Hart, who, for once found it unnecessary to giggle. Instead, she smiled with her lips tightly shut, and drifted her eyes from Edmund to Violet as if it was vivid exercise. Edmund, realizing his mistake, cleared his throat, and offered a polite greeting in a more indifferent tone.

"Miss Violet. Good of you to join us." Mrs. Langley added, with a greeting much less enthused than her brother in-law. Her words were polite, but Violet sensed a forced nature to her pleasantries. Mrs. Langley pursed her lips as she looked Violet up and down. "What a lovely gown."

"Indeed, such fine muslin has been used," Ms. Hart said, feeling Violet's skirts between her pale fingers. "I did not think a governess could afford such things!"

Violet was taken aback by this sentiment. She wondered how Ms. Hart had the audacity to inquire upon Violet's finances. The discomfort of the night was already beginning and they hadn't even begun dinner yet.

"It was a gift from my late father." Violet explained. She dared a look at Edmund, who stared at her with that faraway expression of his. She wondered what he was thinking of.

A few more uncomfortable moments passed with her hosts, until finally, dinner was announced to be ready. Alfred Langley, who had been generally quiet until now, commanded that they ought to travel into the dinning room.

It was an odd feeling to sit at the Langley's massive dining table, which filled much of the room. Violet was instructed to sit across from Mrs. Langley, likely so the woman could critique her edicate. It had been a long time since Violet had eaten in the presence of others, and thus hoped her manners would not be offensive. She took a small bite of the first course, and chewed quietly.

"So, Miss Violet, how old have you turned today?" asked Ms. Hart.

"Two and Twenty," Violet said.

"My, I should have thought you older than that," Ms. Hart mused, seemingly innocent to the rudeness of her words. Violet was flustered at this comment, and she felt her cheeks reddening. "I am terribly fearful of aging ungracefully, myself. How I wish I might stay this young forever. I feel as though I can do anything in my youth!" Ms. Hart continued.

"Ms. Hart will age beautifully, I am quite certain. Will she not?" asked Mrs. Langley. By her rather expectant gaze at Edmund, Violet reckoned the question was directed towards him. All eyes turned on Edmund, who sat next to Violet. He seemed to fit the massive wooden dining chair which he sat in, with its tall back lining his own lengthy frame.

"Oh, uh, yes, of course," Edmund replied. "I believe all three of you fine ladies shall age with grace." Violet felt his eyes fall on her, if only for a moment. Mrs. Langley and Ms. Hart seemed satisfied enough by Edmund's answer, and moved on in subject.

"Now, Miss Violet, do you plan to ever settle down? Begin a family of your own? You seem to dote on the Langley children so." Ms. Hart asked, returning her attention to Violet. Violet's stomach seemed to twist and turn at the subject, which she reckoned was what utter dread felt like. Between Alfred and Katherine Langley, she least expected Ms. Hart to be the one to, unintentional as it might be, to thrust uncomfortable questions upon her. When Violet had told Edmund about her past and future ambitions, it had felt natural and congenial. But she did not wish to speak of such intimate things to that of the Langleys and Ms. Hart. Yet, she had to answer to some extent.

"I do dote on Charlotte and Freddy. They are such amiable children," Violet started. "But having a family of my own is unlikely in my current--situation in life."

Ms. Hart cooed a sympathetic tone and tilted her head like a puppy dog. Violet was not certain if it was this reaction which burned her cheeks due to embarrassment, or the fact it was a reminder Violet's future was to be a spinster. No matter how much she slowly gave her heart to Edmund, there was no possibility of any future with him.

"I find myself in a similar situation, Miss Violet," Edmund said. It was as if he could read her thoughts, and see her discomfort. Every tiny look, every subtle movement, seemed to console Violet, or at least attempt to. His remark certainly took attention away from her. Mrs. Langley stiffened and pursed her lips.

"Do explain," Mrs. Langley said.

"Well, my current professional ambitions are at the forefront of my focus, much like Miss Violet. I plan to complete my last term in Oxford and pass my physician's exam before I take a wife."

"Must you make me wait for such a time to see a Mrs. Edmund Langley? I am very much in need of another lady in this family."

"I thought you enjoyed the attentions of being the only Langley lady," Alfred Langley muttered. He had been rather quiet all night, and took occasion on interjecting their conversations. Unfortunately for him, Mr. Langley's sentiments were not received well by Mrs. Langley, who glared at him coldly.

"Contrary," Mrs. Langley said. "I am quite willing to share the Langley name to a young lady who deserves it."

"Oh?" Mr. Langley said. Though he had already lost interest in the conversation. He sat at the head of the table and tipped his glass all the way back, dripping the last droplets of port down his throat.

"Every gentleman needs an accomplished wife by his side. Her good qualities certainly impart on his, and can either shame or elevate his family name. And thus, a Langley woman must come from a respected family, and be well educated and accomplished. And she must carry herself with an air which exudes elegance and class."

"Well, I am willing to wait on a wife for now. Such a task seems rather daunting in your phrases," Edmund said with an awkward chuckle. Violet stared intensely at her plate, not trusting her expression to look at Mrs. Langley or Edmund.

"Nonsense," Mrs. Langley countered. "There are many accomplished ladies nearby who would fit the Langley name well." Mrs. Langley's eyes slid to the direction of Ms. Hart, ever so subtly.

Like Ms. Hart.

It was entirely obvious that Isobella Hart would make the perfect Mrs. Edmund Langley. She was young and beautiful, and likely very accomplished. No doubt she came from a wealthy, amiable family, and had been trained from a very young age how to be a charming wife and lady of society. Violet knew in her head that Ms. Hart would, should, become Edmund's wife. And it pained her greatly to think of such. The thought had crept into her mind before, in fact it came every time she saw Ms. Hart and Edmund together. However, hearing Mrs. Langley speak of what a Langley woman must be finally showed her the realities of the situation.

How had Violet let herself become so attached to Edmund Langley? Her affection for him had crept into her heart, and she knew not what should be done of it.

Violet swallowed hard and took a deep breath, willing herself to be strong and hold back her tears. She needed to leave.

"I--I do not wish to seem ungrateful--for this lovely dinner," Violet started. Her voice was meek and shaky. It took a few moments to gain her companions' attention. Mrs. Langley almost looked as though she had forgotten that Violet was even at the table. But the surprise of her wavering voice lead to a trickling of silence, and focused eyes on Violet.

"But, I must ask to be excused," Violet continued. "I suffer from a headache, and think it best if I retire to my room early--if that is acceptable?"

All was quiet; Mr. Langley looked up from his newly refilled glass of port and nodded at Violet. For good measure he raised his hand in a dismissive motion, causing Violet to release a breath of relief. She forced a polite smile and rose from her chair, triggering everyone else to rise as well. Violet curtsied and turned on her heel, trying her best to escape the dining room in an acceptable amount of speediness.

Her heart pounded and her breathing fluttered quickly as she tried to suppress her tears. Instead of retiring to her room, Violet decided to find solace in the gardens. She burst out of doors and ran a few paces, so she was among the flowers. Breathing in their sweet scent, she finally let herself weep. Was this what heartbreak felt like? Violet reckoned it felt like how she imagined heartbreak to be.

"Violet!"

Violet whipped around to see Edmund running towards her, with great concern in his countenance. She quickly wiped the tears from her cheeks, but it was no use. Her red, shiny eyes spoke loudly to Edmund. He stopped merely inches away from her, in a closeness both painful and welcomed by Violet.

"You've been crying," Edmund said in a quiet surprise. He raised one of his strong hands, and with some hesitance, gently caressed the side of her face. Violet opened her mouth, but found she could not speak.

Edmund caught a falling tear with his thumb.

He need not say anything and nor did she, if she could, feel the need to explain herself. It was as if he already knew why she was upset. He always seemed to understand her, when no one else cared to even try. Violet looked up at him, and noticed he had somehow moved closer to her. His dark eyes stayed steadfast on her own, watching, waiting for Violet's permission as he placed his other hand on her face, and slid both sets of fingers down her jawline, until they clung to the nape of her neck.

Violet stood motionless, unable to do much of anything but focus her attention on Edmund. His touch gave her goose-pimples, yet also somehow seemed to warm her. His black eye, which had turned swiftly into a soft yellowish brown, was barely visible in the tinted light. Edmund's eyes began flickering to her lips, much like the last time they were in the hedge maze together. She did the same, wondering what it might feel like to be kissed by him, if only once. She would find out soon enough.

Edmund closed the gap between them and pressed his lips against Violet's. It was soft and sweet, and it sent a rush down Violet's spine. So many thoughts and feelings rushed into her heart at once, but Violet kept only the amiable ones.

Edmund pulled back, if only a little, so he might catch his breath.

"Happy birthday," he whispered. They beamed at each other, both incandescently joyful. So joyful, in fact, that neither of them seemed to notice the figure, which lingered by one of the large windows of the Langey home. The window, which held such a clear view of the couple embracing one another.

Chapter Twelve

"It is just as we suspected, I fear," Edmund said to his brother. He set the letter down with a forceful slap of his hand. Alfred stood with his arm on the mantle of the fireplace and sighed. Some time had passed since the two had last fought, when events had spiraled into a physical nature. As such, Alfred and Edmund had moved on and were once again on speaking terms. It was the natural pattern of the Langley brothers: to argue and mend, in a rather quick succession.

"Mr. Andrews says your gambling debts are valid, and if you were to deny them, it would likely result in a challenge to a duel," Edmund continued. His old friend from boarding school had finally returned his letter in regards to Alfred's debts. He had hoped the eyes of a lawyer would give the situation some hope, yet it seemed to have the reverse effect. "Because your only options are to pay your debts or surrender your estate to Lord Albey, Mr. Andrews suggests attempting to form some relationships with your debter. Perhaps you might be able to come to a less threatening agreement with Lord Albey, such as a longer timeline to pay your debt."

"This Mr. Andrews truly believes that becoming friendly with Albey, will somehow cause him to forget of my debts? Rubbish, I say." Alfred scoffed.

"That is not what he means. But it certainly cannot hurt to get into the good graces of Lord Albey."

"No, I suppose not."

The muffled sound of giggling children caught Edmund's attention, causing him to rise from chair and turn towards the window. Outside, Violet was picking flowers with the children, and collecting them in a basket. Edmund watched as Violet tickled the back of little Freddy's neck with a daisy, causing the boy to scrunch up his neck and laugh. Edmund found himself grinning at this and wishing he was with them. His eyes focused on Violet, starving for her company, for her touch. Perhaps it was ungentlemanly of Edmund to have kissed her the night before last, having not yet an official understanding with her. But Edmund could not help himself. That dinner had been less than pleasant, with Ms. Hart's passive insults and Mrs. Langley's opinions on the ideal Mrs. Edmund Langley. But it had caused him to think of his future, if only a little. And he was beginning to realize that he was in love--true, deep love, with Violet.

"What do you think of it?"

Alfred's question cut through Edmund's thoughts and pulled his attention back on his brother. Edmund turned away from the window and looked blankly at Alfred. He had completely missed what Alfred had been rambling about, and now was unsure of what to say.

"I--come again?"

Alfred, clearly irritated he had to repeat himself, rolled his eyes and took a swig of brandy before replying.

"The Browns are having a private ball in a few days. Lord Albey is likely to attend. I might speak to him then."

"That is a splendid idea." Edmund said.

"And you will come, as well?" Alfred asked. There was a slight hopefulness in his tone, as if Alfred wished for his brother's support.

"Certainly," Edmund said in earnest.

The brothers nodded at each other in a silent understanding. For the moment, all was good between them, and Edmund hoped it might last longer than the last time.

*

Violet was in a state of undeniable euphoria and happiness. She could not help but think of Edmund at nearly all times of the day. She felt like a giddy child, taking too much pleasure in everything around her. And she minded not. The night before last, Edmund had proved his affections for her grew deeper than friendship. He had kissed her. And in doing so, Violet felt that perhaps there was some hope for a future with him. She knew soon the realities of that hope would eventually attack her, as they always did. But at the moment, such thoughts were left clawing at her, with little success. Violet reveled in her reverie, hoping one day it might be her reality.

Humming quietly to herself, Violet slowly made her way to her bed chamber. The day was already ending, and soon she would take her dinner in the solitude of her room. It was not long until she made it to her bed chamber. Violet, still in a daze of felicity, grabbed the thick doorknob, turned, and pushed, in a familiar motion that had been repeated many times.

All humming and daydreaming stopped, however, at the sight of who stood inside her chamber.

"Mary," Violet said. She tried to sound indifferent, and not exclaim the maid's name in the fearful tone she truly felt. But even still, her voice sounded shaky. Violet did not trust this woman. "Have you come to bring dinner?"

"'Fraid not," Mary replied. "I came on a bit of business, actually." She smiled knowingly at Violet, as if they were both privilege to the same secret.

"What kind of business?" Violet asked. She closed the door behind her, but moved no closer to Mary. The maid smirked, revealing a single dimple on her cheek.

"We'll get to that," Mary said. She looked over her shoulder briefly, as if making sure no one was behind her, even though the two women were clearly alone. "Ye lied to me last time we spoke."

"Did I? And how is that?"

Mary scoffed with a patronizing air and rested her fingers on the metal foot end of Violet's bed. They were like fingers of a skeleton--long and thin, boney sticks, with only a pale covering of skin protecting them.

"Ye said there be nothin' between ye and Mr. Edmund Langley, but that ain't truc, ain't it?" Mary said. Violet's heart began to pound, like a fist trying to punch out of her rib cage. What was Mary getting at?

"I know not what you speak of, Mary. Now, if you wouldn't mind leaving--

"I saw ye two kissing outside the night before last. Saw it plain as day out the window, so don't even try denyin' it."

Mary's black eyes seemed to sparkle at the sight of Violet's face growing pale. Violet suddenly felt sick and queasy. How had she and Edmund been so careless? Their embrace had been a thing of the moment, with no thought other than what the two were feeling towards each other.

"And what does this matter?" Violet asked. Realising she had been nervously fiddling with her fingers, Violet quickly pulled them away and hung her hands by her side, in tight fists. She tried with all she had so stay strong, at least on her outer appearance. She bit her inner cheeks and relaxed her eyes, in the hopes of looking indifferent to Mary's words.

"Well, I'd think Mrs. Langley would find this bit of information mighty interestin', don't ye?"

"You have no proof of anything. Why would she believe anything you say to her?" Violet said. Mary began tapping her skeleton fingers on the bed's foot end. Each tap echoed a metallic note, distracting Violet from the mad's confident smirk. It was quite unsettling, how much this young woman smiled, clearly enjoying the misery she was causing Violet.

"Bringing her attention to the way Mr. Langley looks at ye and ye 'im, would be enough, I reckon. But for good measure, I got this," Mary said. She pulled out a small note from the pocket of her apron.

A gasp escaped Violet's lips. She immediately recognized it as the note that Edmund had put in her bible. Instinctively, Violet scurried to her bedside and thrusted her hand under her pillow. Her fingers clawed at the mattress underneath, searching for the note she knew was no longer there.

"I'm sure Mrs. Langley will find it curious as to why her brother-in-law wished to meet with her governess in the garden at dusk--am I wrong?"

"What do you want, Mary?" Violet barked. The maid gave one last tap of her fingers in an odd excitement.

"A business deal, of sorts."

"What would this business deal entail?" Violet asked, though she reckoned she knew where Mary was heading.

"In return for me keepin' my lips shut 'bout ye and Mr. Langley, I'll be needin' some payment."

Violet sighed. "How much payment will be needed?"

"Oh, ten shillings a week should suffice."

"Ten shillings? That is the amount of compensation the Langleys pay me each Sunday!"

"And?"

Violet was beginning to physically shake. She could not give all of her earnings away to Mary. Her Mama needed that money to live on. Without it, she would surely suffer. And yet, if she didn't give it to Mary, Violet would certainly be out of a position.

"Mary, I am given 20 pounds a year for my position, I am not as wealthy as you might think."

"It be more than I make," Mary said lacking any tone of sympathy . "But the choice is yours. Pay me to keep quiet and ye keep yer position and yer Mr. Langley, or refuse and lose both."

In two swift motions, Mary had made her way to the door, and had her hand on the doorknob. Before leaving Violet's bed chamber, she craned her neck back to meet Violet's gaze.

"I'll give ye until this time tomorrow to make yer decision," Mary said. The door shut behind her with a loud thud as Violet was left alone. How quick her happy reverie had been ripped away. All thoughts of Edmund's lips were no match for the thoughts which faced her now.

Violet knew not what to do. She could not simply abandon her mother--she needed to support her. And yet, if Violet's relationship with Edmund was discovered by Mrs. Langley, her reputation would be in shambles. If such a scandal broke out, Violet might not be able to acquire another position, after Mrs. Langley most assuredly would throw her out. It was an impossible situation.

Violet collapsed on her bed with a defeated thud, and rested her fiddling hands on her stomach. She stared at the ceiling, which Violet realized held many cobwebs in the corners. She startled when a knock on her door offered dinner, but she declined. Violet at quickly lost her appetite.

Chapter Thirteen

Violet felt ill. The kind of ill which felt like assault on her stomach, wounding it with a bleed of nausea. She could not stop her skin from shivering, despite the absence of chill in the air. It was all the cause of Mary and her threats. She did not, could not, sleep a wink last night, for Violet's mind was much too preoccupied with worries of what to do. As each hour ticked away, her deadline drew nearer. And yet, Violet still knew not what to do. Should she give Mary her wages? Or risk the exposure of her relationship with Edmund?

Oh Edmund.

Violet knew one thing, and that was that she could not tell Edmund of any of this. His thoughts and worries were to deal with his brother's debts, and not Violet's.

Violet reckoned some fresh air would do her good, so she took the children into the gardens for some exercise.

"Can we play chase?" Fredric asked Violet, as soon as they were released into the outdoors. His face was bright with a playful grin, already preparing to run as fast as he could. Violet's heart sank, knowing what she would have to tell them.

"I fear we cannot. Your Mama has informed me that if I am to take you outside for exercise, it must only be for a constitutional."

"But why?" Charlotte moaned.

"It is the only dignified form of physical activity. Apparently."

Charlotte and Fredric's faces fell considerably. Charlotte's eyes narrowed and turned a darker shade of blue--a phenomenon which only happened when she was about to challenge something.

"But what of cricket? Or fencing? Are those not considered dignified physical activities?" Charlotte asked, knowing very well that her own Papa partook in such sports.

"Are you suggesting we fence?" Violet asked with an amused smile, trying to lighten the conversation.

"Yes, let's!" Fredric chimed in, with sparkling eyes. The boy loved a good sword fight, as any young boy did.

"Children, let us not challenge your Mama's wishes. A nice walk about the gardens will do us all some good."

Charlotte rolled her eyes and sighed dramatically, but complied nonetheless. The trio began walking through the gardens, with a silence none were used to when in each others' company. Little Freddy pouted and dragged his feet from behind, clearly heartbroken their exertion would not include any form of running or swashbuckling swordplay. Violet tried to enjoy her surroundings, as they usually comforted her, but she found her efforts in vain. The warm August air seemed too hot, and the sun too bright. She walked with discomfort, causing sweat to moistened her brow. Her dress felt heavy, as if it was holding her down against her own will. But she continued walking.

Violet quickened her pace and entered the hedge maze, feeling the children's presence from behind. There was no logical thought on where they should go in the maze. She simply turned down whichever pathway she saw first, and the children followed. Violet made a sharp turn around a hedge wall, as her mind drifted back to Mary's threats.

Then, down the long pathway, with tall hedges on either side. She reached the end and turned left, then right, then--

As she rounded the corner of a hedge, Violet collided with Edmund. As they crashed into each other, she felt her foot stepping on Edmund's. Though he should have been the one to yelp, it was Violet who let out an exclamation.

"Edmund! You startled me!" Violet cried.

"And you're standing on my foot," Edmund said. Violet looked down at their feet, which were tangled closely together.

"I'm so sorry, I--

"It is no matter. I am glad I've found you alone. I was hoping we could speak--

"But we are not alone." Violet said. Edmund furrowed his brows and looked past Violet.

"Aren't we?"

Violet turned her head, expecting to see Charlotte and Fredric behind her, but alas, they were not. All that was in her sight were the sharp green angles of the hedges.

"Oh blast, I've lost the children," Violet said, her words beginning to tremble. "This is the second time I've lost them." Her thoughts drifted to when Edmund had taken the children outside to play, and Violet had panicked when she knew not where they were. She was beginning to feel the same sense of fear, pounding through her veins.

"It will all be well," Edmund said softly. "I can hear their chatter somewhere through the leaves." He chuckled, taking a moment to listen to the muffled voices of Fredric and Charlotte. They were, indeed somewhat close. But, when Violet's countenance did not change, Edmund took her trembling hands and wrapped them in his sturdy grip. It was instant comfort, but it in turn, weakened her ability to hide her worries.

"Violet, look at me. Something else is the matter. What is it?" His eyes were so full of concern for her as they fought to meet Violet's eyeline.

"Nothing is the matter," Violet fibbed. It wasn't the truth, but it was best if Edmund didn't know the truth. He narrowed his eyes, as if he did not believe her, but pressed her no more.

"Violet, I wish you to know that I--

"Uncle!" Fredric exclaimed, appearing suddenly around the corner, with Charlotte quietly behind. Violet startled, feeling as though she had been caught doing something wrong. Her fingers quickly slipped out of Edmund's grasp. She felt Charlotte's eyes drifting curiously from Violet to Edmund. Her heart quickened, fearing what was in the little girl's thoughts. Violet scurried over to the children. It was best to create as much space from Edmund as possible, she reckoned.

"Children, hello!" Edmund said, a little too enthusiastically. Violet felt his gaze fixated on her, but she could not lift her eyes to him in return. If she did, she feared what she might tell him, even through a simple look.

"Well, I'll leave you three in peace," Edmund said.

"No, walk with us!" Fredric commanded. He ran up to his uncle and tugged at him.

"I fear I need to make my way back to the house. Perhaps another time," Edmund said simply. He bowed his head slightly at Violet, before strolling past and disappearing behind a hedge. Fredric pouted his lower lip even more than it already had been, and sadly took Violet's hand. How the little boy did so dote on his uncle.

*

An hour or so later, Violet and the children were retired in the school room, studying Shakespeare. Violet was reading a passage from 'A Midsummer Night's Dream', in a fog of mindlessness. They sat near the only window in the room, so the natural light could stretch through, onto the pages which she read. As she quietly spoke Shakespeare's words to the children, Violet's eye caught movement out the window. Her eyes slid from the book in her hands to the figure, whom she saw outside. Of course it was Edmund.

She admired him, and his strong, handsome build, which was still evident even from such a distance. He appeared to pacing, with a countenance rather vexed. He ran his fingers through his hair and turned sharply, as he strode back another few steps.

"Violet, read! Why have you stopped?" Freddy cried suddenly. Violet drew her focus back to the children, realizing she had stopped reading the moment her eyes fell on Edmund.

"Oh, ehm--where was I?" Violet said, eyes scanning the script. She felt her cheeks flush, particularly when Charlotte looked out the window, down at Edmund, then back at Violet with a smile.

"Tell me Violet, will you marry Uncle Edmund?" Charlotte asked, her tone with utter casualty. Violet looked at Charlotte in shock.

"Whatever can you mean, Charlotte? What a silly thing to say."

"But you clearly love him, do you not? And he you."

Violet knew not what to say at this. She was completely taken aback by this six-year-old's interrogation, whom, Violet reckoned, was much too mature for her age. Had she been that transparent with her feelings for Edmund that even Charlotte could see it?

Thankfully, Fredric was not as aware of such affairs. He gently tugged the book from Violet's grasp and began examining the pages. His eyes narrowed in concentration, as if a fierce enough stare would enable him the skill of literacy.

"I am young, but I am not stupid. I see the way you look at each other. It is the look of love, or what I imagine love to be. And I saw your embrace in the hedge maze today."

Violet could feel herself sweating at the threat of Charlotte knowing her secret. It was too much of a risk for anyone to know, even dearest Charlotte.

"Charlotte, it is all very. . .complicated."

"I wish you to become my aunt. I believe that would be very splendid, do you not?" Charlotte smiled sweetly, exposing a gentle dimpled cheek. Violet took the girl's small hands in her own and rubbed the tops with her thumbs.

"I do," Violet whispered, with a weak smile. "But my dear, you must know I am your family's servant. I--I am below Edmund's station, and some. . . people. . .would object."

"My parents," said Charlotte. The girl looked down sadly, causing one of her blonde curls to fall across her eyelid. Violet sighed.

"Yes, but not just them. Many people would not like us together, and that creates difficulties. Do you understand?"

"You're like Hermia and Lysander. Forbidden, so you must run away and marry in secret." Charlotte's eyes sparkled as she spoke in her romanticized way. Violet let out a small chuckle, somewhat impressed the girl had referenced 'A Midsummer Night's Dream'.

"In a way. But, dearest Charlotte, Edmund and I have not yet... spoken of marriage. And until we decide what we are to become, we need to keep our affections for one another a secret."

"Do not worry, I can keep a secret, you can trust me." Charlotte said boldly. She straightened in her seat and lifted her chin, as if trying to prove her mature abilities. Violet hated herself for asking an innocent child to keep her secret, but she felt it had to be done. She trusted Charlotte's discretion, and a part of her almost felt relieved that another soul knew of her relationship.

Fredric was still pretending to read the play, clutching the heavy book with his tiny fingers. Violet doubted he was paying attention to her conversation with Charlotte, and decided all would be well for a little while longer.

"I can help you hide your romance with Uncle--I'll do whatever you need."

"What would I do without you?" said Violet with a smile. She rubbed the back of her index finger down Charlotte's rosy cheek affectionately. Violet had a sudden urge of hope, that perhaps she and Edmund could have a life together. In that moment, she decided she would pay Mary's blackmail. She would find a way to continue to send money to her mother--somehow. But she knew she couldn't risk the exposure of her relationship with Edmund. Not yet, anyway.

As soon as the children went to bed and Violet's duties for the day expired, she grabbed her small pouch, which held the week's wages. She gripped the punch tight enough to cause her knuckles to whiten, and scurried out of her room to find Mary. She would not sit and wait until Mary's deadline, waiting, like a scared child, for Mary to arrive. No, she would hunt the woman down and deal with her before Violet could regret what she was doing.

Violet walked quickly down the corridor, feeling a surge of unexpected bravery. She turned the corner, and bumped into Edmund, who had been walking at a similar speed. Violet instinctively put her hands in front of her, as Edmund's chest crashed into them.

"Goodness, Edmund, we must stop meeting like this!" Violet said with a laugh.

"I could think of worse ways to meet," he said. "Although that pouch you're holding has made quite a blow to my chest." Violet drew her hands close to her and twisted the top of her pouch.

"It seems I cannot help but injure you today. First stepping on your foot, now hitting you with my wages!"

"It is no matter," Edmund said. "Incidentally, I have been wishing to speak with you all day." He seemed urgent in his tone. "Is there any chance we may speak?"

Violet looked down at the pouch in her hands, which felt heavy in anticipation of what she was to do with it.

"I apologize, I have something I must take care of. Afterwards, I'd be happy to speak with you. But I really must go."

Violet stepped forward, as if to pass Edmund, but thought better of it. She did not want Emdund to think her as indifferent to him. So, in all her boldness, she leaned into him and kissed him gently on the cheek. It was a swift motion, barley a brush against his skin. But it was proof of her affection for him. Edmund stared at her, lips curled up, and watched wordlessly as she passed him. Violet's cheeks burned, feeling the reality of what she had just done, but she smiled to herself. She was in love with Edmund; she could admit it to herself with an openness she never before had. Even with no official understanding between them, Violet felt a surge of hope. Blackmail and opposing classes--could they really keep Violet and Edmund apart, if they truly loved each other?

It was not that difficult for Violet to find Mary. She was sitting at the old wooden dining table in the servant's quarters, smoking a cigar she likely had stolen. When Mary caught Violet's figure in the doorway, she smirked and let out a blow of smoke in her direction. Violet narrowed her eyes and stifle a cough.

"Ms. Violet," Mary said. "Fancy seein' you here, down in the servants quarters." Her tone dripped of a loathing Violet could not quite understand, but she could return it.

"I've come to pay you, to keep quiet about Edmund and I."

Mary smiled greedily and sucked on her cigar.

"Splendid," Mary said. She rose from her seat and meandered up to Violet. Mary reached out to grab the pouch from her, but Violet pulled it away.

"You know, I think it's disgusting what you're doing. I still don't understand how you could do such a thing to me." Violet said.

"The privileged never understand."

Mary blew a puff of smoke onto Violet's face. It took all of Violet's might not to cough violently, as she was not used to breathing in such a smell. But one thing she would not do was let herself appear weak in front of Mary. She allowed herself one small cough, and stifled the rest.

"Well, you better keep quiet if I'm giving you my wages. If I find you've breathed a word to anyone, I will stop payment immediately."

"Obviously," Mary scoffed, finally grabbing the bag of money from Violet's hands. "My lips be sealed." She looked inside, as if checking to make sure the bag did contain Violet's wages.

"I'm sure you'll find everything is in order, to the exact amount you require," Violet said. She crossed her arms, suddenly feeling sick. Mary nodded and stuffed the bag into the pocket of her crisp white apron.

"Just hope it's worth it for ya. Ye know the word among the other servants, is that yer precious Mr. Edmund Langley had quite a scandal when he be livin' back in Oxford."

"Oh?" was all Violet could manage to say. Her breathing went shallow at the mention of Oxford. She had overheard Edmund speaking to his brother about some secret surrounding Oxford, but he had never mentioned it to her. She had always quietly wondered what had happened there, but daren't ever ask.

"Word has it he got in his cups and attacked one of his classmates. Nearly killed the man, from what I hear, and would've been thrown out of physician's college, if it weren't for his brother."

Violet said nothing. She only stared at Mary's smug countainance, trying to determine if the maid was being truthful. She could not trust the young woman. She could plainly see the cracks of Mary's morality, like the folds of her skin. Yet deep down, Violet felt there might be truth to her words.

"That's quite a story," Violet said. That was all she would say on the subject, as Violet refused to give Mary the satisfaction of rattling her. "I trust you will not bother me again until my next payment is due."

Mary puffed another bit of smoke and nodded. She sat back down at the servant's table. Without her cap on, her slicked black hair shone under the brief candlelight. Her back turned towards Violet, signalling their business was done. With a growing sickness in her stomach, Violet turned on her heal and sped through the hallways of Langley manor. She felt a sickness quickly crawling up her throat. Her steps quickened with urgency as she threw herself out the front door, and found the nearest shrub to release her sickness upton. Violet bent over, clutching her stomach and clawing at it, as she vomited. She wasn't sure if this sickness came from what Mary had said about Edmund, or from giving the wretched woman her wages, instead of her mother. Or perhaps it was simply from the cigar smoke. Whatever the cause, mattered not. Violet coughed up the last of her vomit, and breathed the fresh summer air into her lungs. The after-affects of such a sickness stung her throat as she swallowed for the first time.

Could Mary have been truthful in her stories of Edmund? Violet could not find a proper reason for her to fib about it, other than tormention. Not that Mary was above that, she reckoned. Still, violence in a drunken rage was not out of characteristic for a Langley man. Could Edmund be the same?

Violet's stomach felt heavy, despite being just emptied. What truly happened in Oxford?

*

Edmund tried not to frown as the carriage pulled away from the Langley's estate. Katherine and Alfred sat across from him, respectively overdressed and under-enthused. Edmund had not the chance to speak with Violet before leaving for the Brown's ball. He had wished to converse with her about what had happened the night of Violet's birthday. Edmund wanted to confess his feelings to her once and for all, so they might have an official understanding. He found himself quite in love with Violet, and he was tired of being tentative about it.

Unfortunately, every time Edmund bumped into Violet, it seemed she had a prior engagement. Now, Edmund would have to endure a long night out, while anticipation simmered inside him. It would be at least another day before he might speak with dear Violet.

"I do hope the displeasure painted on both of your faces will vanish before we arrive at the ball. Such festivities are meant as a pleasurable experience, you realize?"

Edmund looked at Katherine, the slight expression of surprise hiding in his eyes. He felt Alfred shift in his seat with discomfort.

"Forgive me, sister. I was nearly deep in thought. I reassure you, I am quite looking forward to tonight." Edmund said, forcing a smile. Katherine seemed satisfied with his answer, and whipped her head in the direction of her husband. In doing so, the ostrich feather which sat erect in her hair, licked the side of Alfred's face. He said nothing, but sighed with a dark tone of defeat.

"And you? What is your reason for being so miserable tonight?"

"You know I am not one for large crowds of people. It causes me distress more than anything."

"Ah yes, how could I have forgotten your natural disdain for humankind?" The sarcasm which dripped from Katherine's tongue felt like it could slice the air. Edmund sat in silence, slightly bewildered. He found it best to stay quiet when Katherine and Alfred had their bitter moments together.

"My disdain runs deeper for some more so than others," Alfred spat, eyeing his wife cooly. "And I am, in fact, looking forward to speaking with certain persons tonight, if that will satisfy you."

Ah yes, Edmund had nearly forgotten the sole reason they were attending this ball to begin with. Lord Albey was certain to be there, giving Alfred the chance to get in the man's good graces. God willing.

The carriage ride seemed to last much too long, and all parties seemed relieved when they finally arrived at the Brown's estate. Women in fine dresses and men in crisp cravats filled the walls of Highford Park. Candles and crystal chandeliers lit the rooms, and cast shadows among the figures. The room was a buzz of stringed melodies and laughter, which Edmund found a pleasant change from the contained aggression that had filled the Langley's carriage ride. He watched as Katherine immediately dissolved into the room; her only identifying feature was the large ostrich feather which seemed to float through the crowd, like a flag billowing in the wind. Edmund took to his brother's side, as they scanned the faces of the other guests.

"Do you see him?" Edmund asked. He glanced at his brother, who seemed to be staring at a gentleman at the other side of the ballroom.

"There," Alfred said. He used his glass of port to motion in the man's direction. When had he gotten a glass of port?

"Let us waste no time then," Edmund said. The brothers began weaving through the hoard of guests to Lord Albey. They walked the perimeter of the room while lines of young ladies and gentleman danced at its center. "Establishing any sort of friendly relationship with him could benefit you. Try not to even mention your debts with him. Tonight is not about bargaining or begging, it's about networking."

"If that is even possible. I fear it is too late to befriend the man I owe my estate to," Alfred mumbled. Edmund chose not to hear his brother's words. Alfred was likely right, but he would not give up hope. All they could do was--

"Mr. Langley!"

A familiar voice beckoned Edmund, causing him to look behind him. There was Ms. Hart, looking radiant in her cream silk gown. It was sprigged with delicate jewels, which somehow failed to weigh down the light material.

"Ms. Hart," Edmund said with a friendly smile. "How good to see you this evening." Ms. Hart beamed, revealing a set of teeth almost as white as the pearl earrings she wore.

"I am happy you are here. It has been so bleak without my friendly companions," Ms. Hart giggled. Edmund glanced back to where his brother had been, though he was no longer close by. It seemed Alfred had made his way over to Lord Albey, but Edmund daren't watch them for too long. He drew his attention back to Ms. Hart, who seemed to have moved closer to his person. She peered over his shoulder and let out some sort of mixture between a groan and a yip.

"Oh dear, it seems as though Lord Hughbert is making his way over to us!" Ms. Hart exclaimed. She began fanning herself very rapidly, as if vexed by her own announcement.

"And this troubles you?" Edmund asked. Ms. Hart snapped her fan shut with her hand, so rapidly, that Edmund feared she had ripped the material.

"Let us call Lord Hughbert an unwelcome suitor of mine," Ms. Hart said, her voice lowered. She gritted her teeth and upturned the corners of her mouth into a forced smile, as the unwelcomed Lord Hughbert approached. He was a tall fellow, and comparatively thin, except for the matter his nose, which protruded from his face with great volume.

"Ms. Hart, there you are! I have been trying to reach you all night, but thus you always seem to slip away before I could get to you," Lord Hughbert said with an overly large smile. He scratched his full, slightly ginger, mutton chops, in a manor that was rather unlord-like.

"Well, it seems you have finally reached me," Ms. Hart said, with less enthusiasm than what was normal for her.

"Thankfully so, as now I might ask for the honor of dancing with you." Lord Hughbert was all full of hope, it was almost difficult to watch.

"Yes, well I am afraid my dance card is nearly full," Ms. Hart said. She seemed stiff in Lord Hughbert's presence, and rather inattentive to him, which surprised Edmund. He always assumed Ms. Hart gave away her giggles and smiles freely, even with someone she did not like. Edmund had always thought her presence to be naturally flirtatious, yet with Lord Hughbert, Ms. Hart seemed polite, at best. "I have already promised Mr. Langley here, this next dance."

Edmund's eyes widened slightly in surprise, not expecting such a fib, or to be brought into the conversation at all.

"Uh, erm, yes, she has promised me the next dance."

Ms. Hart smiled and winked, ever so slightly at Edmund. Edmund extended his arm for her, which she took with her gloved hand.

"I see. Well perhaps I might be honored with the following dance?" Lord Hughbert asked as Ms. Hart began pulling Edmund away.

"Uh, perhaps indeed!" She called, and gave poor Lord Hughbert a swift curtsy. Edmund escorted her onto the dance floor, before separating into their designated lines.

"Thank you for saving me, Mr. Langley, I am forever in your debt!" Ms. Hart giggled. She looked behind her shoulder, as if making sure Lord Hughbert was far enough away not to overhear her.

"I almost feel pity for poor Lord Hughbert; he really is quite fond of you." Edmund said, as he stood across from Ms. hart, waiting for the music to start.

"It is unforgiving of me to say, I know, but I find him dreadfully plain. And I simply cannot bear the presence of plain people, even a Lord."

Strings began to play, and so did the dance. Edmund and Ms. Hart stepped towards each other, then away, following the line of their respective sexes. They came together again, this time meeting their hands together, then away again.

"Lord Hughbert might have a title and wealth, but I doubt he could provide the things I truly find important in a husband." Ms. Hart said. Her eyes did not waver from Edmund's, even when they turned around each other, in the slow motion of their dance. It was almost unsettling.

"But surely, Lord Hughbert cannot be so bad? He seemed like an amiable gentleman."

"You speak of him as if in his defence," Ms. Hart said sceptically. She raised her perfectly arched eyebrow as she took Edmund's hand.

"Certainly not," Edmund said quickly. "I don't know him well enough to defend or condemn him."

"Well, I do. I could never be the wife of a man whose greatest accomplishment was being born into wealth."

"Says the woman who was born into wealth," Edmund said with a laugh. Then he realized what he had said and reddened. "I apologize, that was unfair of me--"

"No, no, you're quite alright. I like a man who can challenge me," Ms. Hart said with a smile. She giggled and weaved around the lady dancing next to her. Edmund was becoming more and more uncomfortable by the minute. And he had an entire half an hour of her until the dance would finish. This would certainly be a long night.

"You seem to judge Lord Hughbert on his wealth and status, and use it as a reason not to like him. Yet, I've found that one cannot choose who one loves," Edmund started. He paused as the dance required him to move away from Ms. Hart. As they made their way back to one another, he continued. "Love cares not for one's station in society. Rich or poor, the life one is born into does not define who they may be."

His mind drifted happily to Violet. Lovely, wonderful Violet, who still knew not how amazing she was. Despite all of her trivials and struggles in her life, she still managed to persevere with love and kindness. She was a truly remarkable woman.

Edmund felt Ms. Hart studying him with a softness in her expression.

"You speak from experience," Ms. Hart said. It was not phrased as a question, but a statement. It took a moment for Edmund to respond. He was not certain how Ms. Hart would perceive his words, but he said them anyway:

"Yes, I do indeed."

When their dance finally ended, Edmund and Ms. Hart made their way back into the crowd of ladies and gentleman. Edmund quickly spotted his brother in the sea of ladies and gentleman, who stood next to Lord Albey. Lord Albey turned slightly to Alfred and said something, to which Alfred nodded. The two stood in silence together, sipping on their drinks and watching the dancers.

Ms. Hart noticed Edmund's stare and followed his gaze.

"Ah, I see your brother is with my uncle."

Edmund furrowed his brows and looked at Ms. Hart in confusion.

"Lord Albey is your uncle?"

"Why yes," Ms. Hart said. She smiled innocently. "Are you acquainted with him?"

Ms. Hart was the niece of Lord Albey. How had he not known this? Edmund was so deep in thought, that her question almost slipped away from him. He stood, watching Lord Albey and his brother from afar, trying to process Ms. Hart's connection.

"Mr. Langley?"

The sound of Ms. Hart's voice pulled him from his thoughts.

"Uh--no, I am not. My brother knows him."

"So it appears," Ms. Hart said, her eyes sliding back to Lord Albey and Alfred. "Well let me introduce you." Ms. Hart took Edmunds arm and gently lead him over to their respective relatives.

"Uncle!" Ms. Hart exclaimed as she approached Lord Albey. He was nearly the same height as Albert, but sported a bulging stomach. Lord Albey smiled and kissed Ms. Hart's cheek. Alfred's eyes widened as he looked from Lord Albey to Ms. Hart, clearly surprised by their connection. He said nothing, however, standing mute by his debter's side.

"Dearest Isobelle, how are you my darling?"

"Splendid," Ms. Hart glanced at Edmund with a grin. "I wish to introduce you to Dr. Edmund Langley, the younger brother of Mr. Alfred Langley, here."

"Though I am not yet a doctor, Ms. Hart."

"Yes, yes, details,"

"A pleasure to meet your acquaintance, sir," Edmund said with a bow.

"Likewise," Lord Albey said. His silver hair was tied back, and he stood with a cane that Edmund could not determine if it was for support or style. Either way, Lord Albey was clearly a man of wealth and class. "I must admit, your name is not unfamiliar to my ears. Ms. Hart mentions your name frequently in conversation."

Edmund's stomach dropped with those words. She spoke of him to her uncle? It was a sign of a deep affection on Ms. Hart's part, certainly. Tonight was the first time Edmund started to consider how Ms. Hart might truly feel of him. Were her affections deeper than flirtation?

Edmund could not think of an appropriate reply to Lord Albey's comment, so he instead forced an awkward chuckle.

"Well, I think I will go make company of your wife, Mr. Langley." Ms. Hart said, glancing up at Albert. She curtsied and turned away in one fluid motion, with much grace. The men watched her leave for a moment, before Lord Albey turned his attention back to Edmund.

"I was just about to go into the backroom for a game of cards. Care to join me?"

Edmund was slightly surprised by this friendliness by Lord Albey. He locked eyes with Alfred, trying to communicate with him silently, but failed.

"I'd be honored." Edmund replied.

"Splendid," Lord Albey said. He turned sharply to Alfred, as if just remembering his presence. "I assume, of course, that you will not be joining us?" His polite question held a deeper meaning that all three men knew, and daren't say.

"No, I best not," Alfred said, taking a swig of his drink. The men parted ways, Edmund following Lord Albey into the backroom, while Alfred likely left to seek out more alcohol.

The backroom was much smaller than the ballroom, and much quieter. The walls were a deep mustered, and were lit by dozens of fresh candlesticks. Several wooden tables scattered about their room, at which sat men of all ages drinking and playing cards. Edmund and Lord Albey found an empty table and sat down together. Before Edmund had time to realize there were no cards on the table to actually play, Lord Albey spoke.

"I am not one to waste time with long winded conversations filled with passivities, so I will speak plainly to you," Lord Albey started. He tapped his chubby fingers on the table, drawing attention to a rather large ruby ring which sat heavily on his pinky. "It has come to my attention recently that my niece is quite fond of you. Extremely fond. I of course, already had a notion of this from the constant upbringing of your name in our conversations. But it was confirmed for me just now, as I watched the both of you dance together. Ms. Hart has had several suitors, even in her young age, and never once has her eyes shone in the way they do when she looks at you."

Edmund's mouth went dry at such a statement. He felt an uncomfortable burning, sparked in the pit of his stomach, and it fed all the way up to his cheeks. Edmund had never truly considered the seriousness of Ms. Hart's attention towards him. Even more alarming, was that he was completely unaware of how his pleasantries toward her might have been perceived. As the bosom friend of Edmund's sister in-law, Edmund was always pleasant and friendly towards Ms. Hart. But, did she misinterpret his politeness as affection? Had Edmund been encouraging Ms. Hart without even knowing it?

Edmund scratched the back of his neck and forced himself to look into the eyes of Lord Albey.

"Ms. Hart is a lovely young lady, but--

"Did you know, my dearest niece is to inherit my fortune and title when I leave this world?"

Edmund furrowed his brows in confusion. Lord Albey narrowed his cloudy grey eyes and raised a bushy white eyebrow, as if studying Edmund's expression.

"You did not know this, did you?" Lord Albey asked. Edmund shook his head. "My wife and I were never were blessed with children, and thus a natural heir. But, my dearest Isobelle has been like a daughter to me, as much as child from my own loins could ever be. And thus, I have appointed her as my sole heir. She will inherit my estate in Hampshire, as well as any fortunes I might require from my debtors," Lord Albey paused, as if emphasizing what that truly meant: If Alfred loses his estate to Lord Albey, the house--and everything else, will eventually go to Ms. Hart.

"I am not certain I understand what you are getting at, my lord." Edmund said. Lord Albey smiled as if he was privy to a delightful secret he just had to tell.

"Ms. Hart is in love with you. I am certain if you asked for her hand in marriage, she would accept. And in her becoming a Langley, your family would no longer be in my debt. Even if I still held your brother to his debts, after I pass--though God willing, I still have a few more years left in me--the money and estate would be back in the hands of your family."

This was all too much for Edmund to bare. He was still trying to accept the mere fact that Ms. hart was indeed related to Lord Albey--let alone his heiress. What was even more curious, was why it seemed Lord Abley was trying to create a scenario which would take away all of Alfred's money problems.

"That would be... ideal," Edmund started. "Yet, I am only the second son of a generally wealthy man, who has never been described as great. I come from a reasonably good family and could be considered as well-bred, yes. But, I am not yet established in my profession, and even when I am, I highly doubt a simple physician would be enough for a woman set to inherit a title in the nobility. Surely I must question why you would approve of such a pairing between Ms. Hart and myself?"

Lord Albey leaned back in his chair and rested his hands on is plump belly. It was the only part of him that was considerably thick, with his legs and arms rather slender and short. The man let out a soft chuckle, and replied, "All very true facts, young man. But who am I to get in the way of young love? Quite frankly I care not for anything but for my niece's happiness. And such happiness lies with you, in her eyes."

It would be so easy. So simple. All of Alfred's financial problems would be solved if Edmund would just marry Ms. Hart. The debts would be dismissed, and Edmund would be attached to a woman set to inherit a fortune. How fortunate such a circumstance it might have been, were it not for the fact he was completely and full-heartedly in love with another woman.

Chapter Fourteen

Edmund bit his inner cheek, trying to think of how he would respond to Lord Albey. The last thing he wanted to do was to offend the man, but there was no way he could ever marry Ms. Hart. No matter how much he wished to help his brother in his financial struggles, he could not bring himself to agree to this.

"Your offer is tempting," Edmund started. "And Ms. Hart is a lovely woman. But I fear I do not equal her affections." Lord Albey raised a bushy eyebrows and frowned.

"My niece is well-bred, well-educated, beautiful, and part of a lofty inheritance. And somehow she loves you more than you her? You do not see her fit to be your wife?" his accusations slapped Edmund with the same force as his cane, which met the hardwood floor in a loud crash.

"No, no! I am sure Ms. Hart will make an exquisite wife for some lucky gentleman. But I am. . . .well, the truth is. . . . I am attached to another." Edmund confessed.

"Attached to another?"

"We are soon to be engaged, in fact."

"Really?" Lord Albey asked with a calm curiosity, as he leaned across the card table. Edmund nodded and let out a breath. He had not realized how good it would feel to confess this to someone other than himself. He was cautious not to expose Violet's name to Lord Albey, as their relationship still breathed in secrecy. But an unlikely wave of pleasure wafted over him at his little confession. Yes, Edmund was attached to another, and yes, he would ask for her hand. It became clearer by the second, so much so, that he had a sudden urge to leave the bloody ball right then, and ride home to do the deed that night. But he knew he couldn't do that, and instead, rose from his seat, ending his conversation with Lord Albey.

"My utmost sincere apologies to you, my lord, and Ms. Hart, for any misunderstandings. But I'm afraid our families cannot unite this way."

Lord Albey rose as well, all the anger taken out of him. The old man only nodded in his disappointment, more in defeat than offence.

"I hope this situation will not affect your dealings with my brother." Edmund said. He meant this an assurance that Lord Albey would not be unfairly harsh on Alfred because of Edmund. And yet, having spoken, it came out much differently.

"Oh I assure you, Mr. Langley, it will not."

*

The night could not end fast enough for Edmund, who passed the time by indulging in mindless polite chatter with acquaintances. He smiled and avoided direct eye contact with the young ladies around him, lest he feel obligated to ask them to dance. Instead he nodded and passed comments about the weather, waiting impatiently for the ball to come to an end. Any other night, Edmund might have been in a mood to enjoy himself, and indulge in the spirits of a decent ball. But all Edmund could think about Violet. And avoiding Ms. Hart.

It wasn't until the early hours of the next morning in which he was permitted to leave. Katherine bid her farewells to the hosts and off they piled back into the carriage. His sister-in-law had barely crossed paths with him all night, and it wasn't until he sat across from her in the cozy carriage, that he sensed something was amiss with her. Her lips were pursed shut, much too tightly, and her eyes had darkened and sharpened.

"Did you enjoy yourself, Katherine?" Edmund asked. Katherine looked out of the carriage window as their carriage surged forward.

"Well enough," Katherine said, her voice clipped. She didn't even bother glancing at Edmund with her reply. Edmund looked at Albert, who sat beside his wife with an unamused expression. He shook his head and rolled his eyes, clearly disinterested in his wife's vexation. Edmund decided not to press on further, but by the time they arrived back at the Langley estate, her coolness towards him had become too much to bear.

"Katherine, is something the matter?" Edmund asked, stopping his sister-in-law, and pulling her into the drawing room.

"What do you very well think?" Katherine spat. She scowled at him and glared at him; her eyes were boiling up with rage, Edmund could see it. Her face seemed to contort into a twisted expression, shadowed and lit by the bright glow of the sunlight, shining through the window. Alfred slumbered past the two in a pointed disinterest. Edmund doubted he would see his brother again until the evening.

"I don't understand," he said dumbly. Katherine scoffed.

"I cannot believe that you would throw away a perfectly good opportunity to save this family from ruin. Really, Edmund, you will never find yourself a better wife than Ms. Hart, or a better way to mend my husband's debts."

Edmund stood, open-mouthed, in disbelief. Katherine knew about Alfred's debt? And Lord Albey's proposal? But how?

"You know of Alfred's debts?"

"Of course I do, I'm not an imbecile. I know my husband, and I know when he is lying to me. I suspected it a long time ago, and waited for Alfred to tell me we were destitute, but he never did." Katherine said, rolling her eyes. She slithered about the room, pretending to admire its trinkets, as if it were the first time seeing them. Something shifted in Katherine's countenance as Edmund watched her, as if a veil had been lifted, and she finally was showing her true face. Her anger seemed to disappear, in its place was a sharp shadow of pride.

"But, what of the lady's maid, that you let go for stealing? Did you know that it was Alfred who took your jewelry?" Edmund felt a burning in the pit of his stomach, afraid to hear the answer.

"Of course I knew! I accused the maid in hopes Alfred would finally confess the truth. But my husband is a selfish coward, who only cares of his own well-being."

"So you kicked out a perfectly innocent maid, with no reference, for a crime you knew she did not commit?"

"I did not say I was entirely innocent. It's a shame really, because it's been dreadful finding a new lady's maid. But we all must make our sacrifices," Katherine said.

Edmund could not believe what he was hearing. He could not believe that he had actually had sympathy for Katherine in Alfred's folly. He had thought that she was a victim, but she was just as twisted in folly as his brother.

"What a wretched thing to do!" said Edmund.

"What a wretched thing to do, was to refuse a proposal to Ms. Hart, who has the power to save us from financial ruin!" Katherine snapped. Her dark eyes shifted back into anger. But so did Edmund's.

"How am I surprised that you knew about such a thing," Edmund scoffed.

"Darling, I was the one who put it all into motion," Katherine said. "You know not how diligently I have worked over the summer? I had to discover who Alfred was indebted to, and when I happily discovered his hair was Ms. Hart, I tirelessly strove to bring you and Ms. Hart together! And to convince Lord Albey that such a union would be agreeable in the first place! I had to insinuate and manipulate, all too carefully. It was exhausting, really."

Edmund knew not who the woman was that stood before him. He certainly had known that Katherine was no angel, but this? This deviance and selfishness was beyond his comprehension.

"Oh please, Edmund, don't look at me like that. It is not as though marriages of convenience and financial benefit are so unheard of. I reckon they happen more than marriages of love. I know mine certainly was for the latter."

"But you did it for your own gain. And you convinced a woman to love me that I can never marry."

"Well perhaps you should. This whole situation could be solved and done with if you marry Ms. Hart," Katherine said. She approached Edmund and stood close to him, staring him down as if trying to read his thoughts. "I'll even rehire that lady's maid that you seem to care so much about."

"This isn't a negotiation, Katherine," Edmund said. He felt sick. Katherine frowned, clearly displeased.

"We'll see about that."

Katherine stormed out of the room, leaving Edmund to process what the entire night's events. His family was quite insane, wasn't it? The Langley fortune seemed to matter less and less the more he thought about it. His family didn't deserve anymore assistance than Edmund had already given them. And he knew now, more than ever, what he needed to do if he wanted to be happy.

Now where was Violet?

Chapter Fifteen

"Word has it he got in his cups and attacked one of his classmates," Mary's words from the evening before rattled around in Violet's mind like a trapped bird. "Nearly killed the man."

How could four little words affect her so greatly?

"Nearly killed the man."

The very thought that Mary's words could be truth pierced her with guilt. It was likely the result of servant gossip, continuously spun and stretched, and retold like a fairy tale. Mary had proven herself as untrustworthy, certainly. And yet, Violet still felt a nagging pinch at the base of her stomach, that perhaps, to some extent, her stories could have truth in it. She knew she needed the truth from Edmund about what happened in Oxford. Yet, she had no idea how to ask him about it without offence.

When the sun finally stretched through Violet's window, she was already dressed and ready to begin the day. The truth was that Violet had awoken before the sun, and spent hours waiting restlessly for it to rise. The Langeys had not arrived back from their ball from the night before, leaving Violet alone with her thoughts, and of course, the children, who still slept soundly in their respective rooms.

Violet decided with the sun freshly in the sky, she could justify beginning her day. The children would not be awake for a few more hours, and Violet had no appetite for breakfast, so she took to the gardens. She found just as much peace in the morning air as she did with the evening, but it was different. The flowers were freshly awaking from the night, and the birds sang the morning in with their soft melodies. Violet took her surroundings in, as she walked through the gardens. She always felt so comforted in the fresh air, as though it possessed healing powers.

The sky was marbled pink and orange, matching many of the flowers which surrounded her. Violet pulled a small knife from the pocket of her apron, and knelt in front of a patch of daisies. She held a daisy stem in her left hand, and sliced the blade through it. Violet carefully laid the severed flower on the grass by her side, as she continued to pick more. She reckoned it was time for a fresh vase of flowers in the school room. The ones which currently sat in the school room's oriental vase were beginning to wilt and die.

By the time Violet had a decent cluster of daisies picked and piled atop one another, the rhythmic sound of carriage wheels and horse's hooves sounded from behind. She craned her neck and watched as it stopped and spit out the Langley family. Mr. Alfred Langley departed from the carriage first, and even from a distance, Violet could see the dark circles under his eyes. His cravat was loose around his neck, likely as an attempt to give him some comfort. She watched as Mr. Langley helped his wife out of the carriage next. Mrs. Langley briefly took his hand as she stepped down onto solid ground. But all within a breath, she marched away with a heated stride, as she clutched her silk shawl closed around her arms. The ostrich feather in her hair shook like an angry finger waving at a child. She appeared to be slightly vexed as she abandoned her male counterparts by the carriage. But then, when was Mrs. Langley not vexed by something or other?

Violet continued to watch the family from a distance, frozen in her own curiosity. She caught her breath when Edmund hopped out of the carriage, looking rather undone in his dark vest and rolled shirtsleeves. His coat draped over his arm, and he carried his tophat with a sturdy grip on its rim. Even in his clear exhaustion from the long night, Edmund looked impossibly handsome.

Edmund strode a few paces behind his brother, watching Mrs. Langley as she lead the way to the great house. Violet tried to wave at him, to attain his attention, but none of the Langleys seemed to notice her standing in the garden. They quickly disappeared inside the house. Not long after Violet heard angry voices shouting from within, likely from the drawing room. The voices were muffled, so she could not make out what was being spoken, but she reckoned it was nothing good. She wondered what happened at the ball to cause such an uproar.

After several minutes the voices died and Edmund burst outside into the gardens. He paused when he caught Violet's stare.

"Good morning," he said, smiling softly. He took Violet's hand and kissed it, much too swiftly to be caught by any prying eyes.

"It seems you have had a long night," Violet mused. Her skin burned where Edmund's lips had just been. She shook her hands and rubbed her palms against her apron, as if trying to wipe off the memory of his touch.

"Much too long for my tastes," Edmund said with a tired smile. "Here, let us walk for a while. I've been wanting to speak with you for some time and have never found the chance."

Violet's heart quickened instantly. She wanted to speak with him as well, but how could she? How could she accuse Edmund of something she didn't even know was true? Her guilt of half-believing Mary's words felt like constant hefty blows to her stomach. All Violet could do was nod and scurry to the cover of the hedge maze--the only place the two were safe together.

Edmund led Violet around the first corner of the maze, so they were no longer visible from the house. He ran his fingers through his dark locks and rested his eyes on her, readying himself for whatever he planned to say next.

"Violet, you must know. . .surely you must know that I am yours entirely," Edmund said. He stood dangerously close to Violet, so close that his hot breath warmed her lips. In a sudden burst, he clutched Violet's hands into his, giving them a quick squeeze of affection. "And as such, I find no other reason to ask you--

"I must ask you something first, if I may," Violet interjected. Her voice wavered with nerves as she watched Edmund's face fall in confusion. She could guess what Edmund wanted to ask her, or at least she hoped she could guess. But something in Violet tugged at her to stop him. She had to know the truth of Oxford, the full truth.

"Will you tell me about Oxford?"

Where Violet's words ended Emund's countenance shifted. His jaw dimpled as he clenched it, and the light seemed to go out of his expression. "It is only that some of the servants have insinuated that you had, a kind of, altercation."

Edmund released his hold on Violet's hands, leaving them to fall, abandoned, on the sides of her worn skirts. He ran his fingers through his hair and took a step away from her. Violet's stomach stung at this shift in Edmund. Had she been mistaken in asking him?

"No, you are right. I should tell you," Edmund sighed, as if answering her thoughts. "It is not something I am proud of, and thus prefer to keep it in the silence of my memories. But you deserve to know." He turned his back to Violet, as if mustering the courage to speak again.

"I was struggling at University when it happened. I like to learn with my hands, by doing, but becoming a physician is largely studying dusty textbooks and passing exams. And then my mother died. She was the only member of my family that I was truly close with. And suddenly she was gone, and I felt guilt for not being there when she passed," Edmund said. His head hung down, as if he was too ashamed to look at Violet. "I was such a wreck that I didn't travel home for her funeral. Instead I poured myself into drink. I suppose a part of me felt that I should have been able save her somehow, to heal her, but of course I know now I couldn't have."

"You are not to blame for her death," Violet said softly, trying to find some comforting words. Her stomach dropped when Edmund finally looked at her, and found tears in his eyes. "Still, I was a broken man, and I started drinking heavily to numb the pain. One night, I had been drinking considerably at a pub, and one of my classmates began taunting me. He said some unsavory things about my mother, which I cannot repeat. But I snapped."

The more Edmund spoke, the heavier Violet's heart felt. She had feared Edmund's violence, like she feared Alfred Langley's violence. But something in her knew Edmund was very different from her brother. He was not the same.

"I beat him. I knew my anger and pain was displaced, but I did not stop--I could not stop--until he was almost unconscious. I am not proud of my actions, Violet, and I want you to know that I have never been in my cups like that since. I--I am not my father." The pain in Edmund's eyes was that of a child's. True and ashamed. Violet wanted nothing more than to embrace him, but she restrained herself. Instead, she closed the distance between them, and grazed her fingertips against his hands. It was her turn to hold them, and kiss them.

"You are not your father," she whispered in agreement. She had never seen him like this, so vulnerable. Usually he was the strong confident one that consoled her.

"That--that is not all," Edmund said. He drew his hands away again, preparing to tell Violet the final blow. "The reason that I owed Alfred--that I felt the need to help his financial troubles more than being a dutiful brother. I told Alfred in a panic what I had done, and he came to London has soon as he had received my letter. He paid off the classmate and everyone in the pub not to report me to the police. I suspect he also paid for silence in keeping it away from Oxford. If they knew what had happened, I would surely have been thrown out of university."

"I see," Violet said softly. It made so much sense, now--Edmund's obligation to Alfred, why, after so many arguments, did he stay by his brother's side, and continue to support him.

"Alfred and I do not have the best relationship, but he was there for me in my time of need, and he brought me out of my slumber. For that I will always be grateful."

"Thank you. I understand now." It was all Violet needed to say. Because she did understand. She thought she would have been bothered more by Edmund's declaration, but she wasn't. It was then that Violet realised how much she really loved Edmund. She loved him for his goodness and his strengths, but she also loved him for his faults. Her Papa used to tell her that love was loving someone for all of themselves. If you cannot love the bad in a person, then you do not deserve to love the good in them.

"Do you forgive me?" Edmund asked. He said this with such hope and fear that Violet could not help but smile.

"There is nothing to forgive. Our pasts should not have the authority to hold on to the happiness of our future."

With those words, Edmund smiled and cupped Violet's face in his hands. He kissed her softly, and in that moment, Violet felt that nothing could stop them.

How naive she was.

Edmund never got to ask Violet his question he had held for her. All too soon, Violet was summoned back to the house, as the children had awoken, and Violet was tethered back to her duties. The day drifted away quickly, as Violet carried herself in a cloud of reverie. Edmund's vulnerability made her feel closer to him, and something in her seemed to burst at their connection. Mrs. Langley even dismissed her early for the evening, telling her that she wished to spend time with the children for herself for the rest of the night. There was so much hope in Violet's heart as she soaked in the quietness of the school room. After dinner Violet had felt too restless to stay contained in her room, so she decided to tidy up the children's study. She put a stack of books back on a bookshelf. A Midsummer Night's Dream caught her eyes, which stuck out slightly in the line of book spines. It made her smile, as it somehow made her think of Edmund. Though in truth, everything made her think of Edmund these days.

"Violet, Mrs. Langley wishes to see you in the drawing room," a footman said, bursting through the door. Violet jumped, surprised at the interruption.

"Oh, thank you Johnny," she said. He nodded and disappeared, leaving Violet by her lonesome once again. A wave of nervous tingles spread up her hands, but she shook the sensation away. Whatever did Mrs. Langley want at this time of night? The children were likely asleep by now.

Her thoughts raced silently as Violet scurried through the halls to the drawing room. She knew something was deeply wrong as soon as she met Mrs. Langley's cold, angered eyes.

"Violet, I am tired and vexed, and thus will keep my speech short and to the point. I have become aware of your incredibly inappropriate relationship with my brother in-law."

Everything in Violet's body went cold.

Chapter Sixteen

"You will pack your things and leave this house with the utmost immediancey," Mrs. Langley commanded. Her features were icy, and dark. Her cheekbones looked concave and shadowed. Her thin mouth twisted into a tight frown as she spoke to Violet like a mother disciplining her child.

"Please ma'am, I beg that--

"Enough." Mrs. Langley halted Violet's words with the wave of her hand. "Your true character has been revealed to me, in your--entanglement--with my brother in-law. Your morals are obviously corrupt, and thus you clearly cannot be trusted to govern my children."

Violet felt her extremities begin to shake, to tremble. Everything she had feared, had worked to prevent, was all coming to her in one swift nightmare. She felt like curling up into a ball and crying herself to sleep, but she couldn't. Her bed was no longer her bed. Her freedom was no longer hers. All she had were her tears, but she would not allow herself to shed them. Not now. Not in the presence of Mrs. Langley.

Alfred Langley sat in silence, and if it wasn't for his grunting softly, Violet would have completely forgotten of his presence. She blinked rapidly, in an attempt to push her tears back in her eyelids. She dared a look at Mr. Langley, who, to her surprise, held an expression similar to that of, could it be, sympathy? His eyes, usually cold, held a soft warmth which Violet had only witnessed in his brother before. Would he say anything? Would he condemn his wife, as he often did? When Violet met those soft eyes, he looked down and shifted in his seat.

No, he would not.

"I've called a coach for you, be grateful for my kindness." Mrs. Langley said. Violet looked down and nodded. It wasn't truly a kindness, but she wasn't about to argue with the woman. A young lady traveling in a public coach at this time of night was borderline dangerous. One never knew what sort of people would be traveling at such a time.

"Might I. . . might I say goodbye to the children before I take my leave?" Violet collected herself enough to look at Mrs. Langley, who only scowled more.

"What udacity you have, girl!" Mrs. Langley shouted, but quickly collected herself. "I believe it best you leave while they sleep. Saying goodbyes would make more. . . complications."

Violet only nodded. She managed to give Mrs. Langley a half curtsy, before bolting to the doorway. She needed to leave before she crumbled in her own misery. But then, suddenly, there was Edmund. She crashed into him, and he held her back, inspecting her pained expression.

"What is going on in here? I heard shouting from the library." Edmund looked to Mrs. Langley, then his brother, both of whom met him with silence.

"They know," Violet breathed. If she wasn't standing so close to Edmund, she doubted he would have heard her. Violet pulled away from him, but Edmund reached out and took her arm. It wasn't an aggressive hold, but a protective one. He rubbed his thumb up and down her arm, in an attempt to comfort her.

"And what of it?" Edmund spat. He bit down on his jaw, causing it to flex.

"You cannot be serious, Edmund," Mrs. Langley scoffed.

"I am quite serious, actually," Edmund said. His fingers loosened around Violet's arm and they slid down to her elbow, as he stepped towards Mrs. Langley. In doing so, Edmund blocked Violet's view of the woman, with his broad shoulders. He was a barrier between Mrs. Langley and herself, like an angry bear, protecting his territory.

"Is it so unimaginable to you that I love Violet? When she is the single most pure and kind and beautiful creature that I have ever known?"

Edmund's words pierced her in the best way that words could. He said them with an urgency and boldness that Violet had never heard before. It was raw, and true. He did love her then. Felicity overtook her countenance, despite all the pain still within her.

"Don't be ridiculous, Edmund, how could you possibly love her?" Mrs. Langley said, her voice like a sharp blade. "She's a servant!"

"She's a governess." Edmund said. It was a statement of a fact, but it felt like more than that. He had said it with pride, as though he was justifying Violet's station.

"Which is barely better than the lady's maid!"

"Whom you framed for a crime she did not commit! Do not speak of the lady's maid to me."

Violet's eyes widened, wondering what Edmund meant by this. She thought that it had been Alfred who framed the lady's maid, not his wife. But now was certainly not the time to inquire.

"The maid was irrelevant, as is Violet! She would not make a suitable wife for you, nor could she save the estate. I will not allow you to throw the Langley name away for this girl!"

"As though you have improved the name yourself,"

"Edmund," Alfred warned. "That is enough." Alfred finally decided to join the argument, now standing up. However, he quickly backed down when Mrs. Langley threw some vile comments at him regarding his inability to be of any use.

"There is no need for you to come to my aid at this point, Alfred. You never have before, and I doubt you would be competent in doing so now."

It was enough to shut the man up, and he sat back down in defeat before he had even truly tried. Violet was surprised. She had always seen Alfred Langley as the vicious, violent one, who snapped at his young daughter for little reason. Who scowled at everything and everyone, and drank himself into an angry slumber. But there he was, sitting in the corner like an obedient puppy, watching his brother and wife argue like agitated wolves. Violet was not certain if she should be impressed or disgusted.

But she was no better. Violet stood behind Edmund in silence, as she let him defend her. She was moved motionless by the shock of it all.

"Katherine, it is not up to you who I marry, and it never will be. Now if you will excuse me, I think we'll be going now," Edmund said, in a tone of finality. He turned back to look at Violet. His face had reddened from yelling, but his expression had softened for her. "Are you all right?"

She wasn't, not really, but it didn't matter. Violet only nodded and swallowed her emotions. Without another word, Edmund led Violet out of the room.

"I'll go collect my things," Violet whispered. Edmund nodded and watched as she scurried away.

It was more difficult than she thought it would be to pack up her things. Violet had made a home out of the Langley house in the few years she had been there. Her room had become just that--hers. Though it was small and shabby, it had been a place of comfort for her.

Violet pulled out her tattered vellise from under her bed, and placed it on top of the cream colored quilt which had kept her warm many winter nights. It did not take her long to pack the few dresses that she owned. When she reached for her violet evening gown, she paused, and held it between her fingers for a moment. That dress now held more memories between its seams than her own mind. What a curious thing memories were. Skewed visions of the past, with both the ability to cause sorrow and joy.

That was enough of that.

Violet quickly shoved the gown into her vellise and closed it. She glanced around the room one last time, so she might remember it: its creaky wooden floors; the small trunk that jammed shut whenever it needed to be opened; the white porcelain vase that rested in the windowsill--it sat there filled with fresh flowers when Violet first came to Langley house, and she would leave it the same. She hadn't realized how much she had come to depend on these things, these constancies in her life. Being a governess was not an easy task, but she had come to love it. And now she was leaving it, leaving the life she had built, leaving the children she had grown to love. Disgraced as a harlot. Violet reckoned if Mrs. Langley had her way, she would ensure no other family would ever take Violet as a governess.

What had she done?

She had done what she had done, and now it was time to leave. Violet picked up her vellise, which was lighter than it ought to be for a collection of one's life possessions, and left her bedchamber. In the hallway, she was met by Mary, who held one of Mrs. Langley's gowns in her hands, likely in need of a mend. For a breath they were silent, both listening to the muffled shouts below. As the yelling grew louder, Mary's expression grew smugger and something in Violet snapped.

"I did everything you asked of me Mary. I gave you my wages and you still had to tell her. Do you realise what you have caused? The entire Langley family is unravelling beneath our feet!" Mary's face quickly fell as Violet took stepped closer to her. She could feel her face reddening with anger. "Have I ever done something ill against you? Or any of the servants, for that matter? Because all I have ever done is try to show you all kindness but all I have ever received in return is a cold shoulder and betrayal. Why do you detest me so? Are you really so heartless as to cause this family to fall in spite of me?" Mary refused to look Violet in the eye but she said nothing. She let Violet shout at her, and with each violent word, Violet felt a strange satisfying release.

"I hope you're proud of yourself, Mary. I know I am not all good, but I know I am at least a better person than you." It was the most unforgiving thing she had ever said to anyone, and it felt so good to say. Violet didn't wait to hear what Mary's reply would be. Instead, she pushed passed the girl and left her in the hallway. Mary's betrayal had left her fuming, but she felt released from it now, if only a little.

When Violet found her way into the foir, she was met with angered voices.

"You're being irrational, Edmund. You cannot leave with her! You're going to tarnish your reputation for this girl! Come, after she leaves, and you have some time without her, we can speak and be rational again." Mrs. Langley's voice echoed against the walls. Edmund scoffed in disgust.

"If Violet is no longer welcome in this house, then neither am I. Besides, I will not let her travel alone at this hour."

The two fell silent and turned to look at Violet as she appeared behind them. She felt like a small child, clinging to her belongings in a timid silence, fearing the wrath of her elders. Edmund's expression softened, as it always did when he looked upon her.

"Good night, Katherine," he said, before taking Violet's arm and escorting her out the front door.

There was only one other passenger in the coach, to Violet's relief. An elderly woman, in tattered muslin and a widow's bonnet, sat across from Edmund and Violet. She had startled when the two had entered, leading Violet to believe the woman had been asleep.

"How lucky I be, to have some company now," the old widow said, studying the two. "And a handsome couple at that!" Even in the dim lighting, Violet noticed the gaping holes in the woman's mouth from missing teeth. She forced herself to smile politely at the woman and she squeezed Edmund's hand tightly. The carriage rumbled forward, and pulled them away slowly from the Langley estate. Violet watched out the window as the gardens passed her; the hedge maze, and the honeysuckle flowers, all gone within a blink.

"Goodbye," she said softly. A tear escaped her eye, and she let it make a path down her cheek and drip off her chin, like rocks tumbling off a cliff. "I'll miss them dearly, you know."

"I know." Edmund replied in a hushed tone. He returned her hand-squeeze with one of his own, and held it in the protective cage of his fingers. She would never see dear little Freddy and bright little Charlotte again. Would they wonder where she was when they woke without a governess? Would they cry in her absence, or would they simply shrug and go play? Violet hoped they would not think she abandoned them because she wanted to. That she no longer cared for them. She hoped they knew she loved them.

Violet turned away from the window, no longer able to watch the Langley estate, and all its contents, run away from her life. She smeared her tears against her cheek and looked to Edmund, suddenly realizing he had not brought any belongings with him in the coach.

"You bring nothing with you," she said.

"I bring you, and that is enough," Edmund said. The old widow let out a sound, which Violet guessed was an endeared "Aw."

"Besides," Edmund continued. "The majority of my belongings are back in London, which we will be arriving in, in a few hours."

"We're going to London?"

"I reckon it's the best place to go to. The only place, really. Besides, I wish you to see my home."

"Is it not scandalous for us to live together unwed?" Violet asked. She was only just beginning to realize what it meant for her and Edmund to run away together. They would be alone together, without the fear of prying eyes. Without the excuse of working. Violet was unsure if the rush she felt in her gut was of excitement, or fear.

Edmund smirked and leaned into her, so his lips tickled her ear.

"Is it not already scandalous for us to love each other?"

"You best be off to Gretna Green, not London, then," the old widow interjected, with an amused smile. This suggestion seemed to please Edmund, who's eyes seemed to sparkle as he thought on this.

"I don't wish to elope." Violet said flatly. She already felt as though her life and morals were spiraling. Her reputation, though not widely known in society, would surely be tainted. Elopement seemed so forbidden, so urgent. It was an unnecessary addition to the scandal of it all. Although living in sin was considerably worse. "I'd like it in a church, with my Mama."

"Very well," Edmund said with a sigh. "You will have your own room at Kentley house, until you become mistress of it."

It was a strange thought, wasn't it? To be mistress of a house, to be a wife. It was a dream Violet had given up on years ago. And yet here it danced in her future, like a forgotten promise, finally coming true.

"I'll spend the night, but I'd like to visit my mother soon." Violet said softly. With all that was happening, she could not process the thought of marriage. She needed to go to her Mama, and ensure she was alright. Though Mary had not blackmailed Violet out of her money for long, she reckoned it was enough to make her mother suffer. As if Edmund heard her thoughts, he said, "I hope you know. . . that your mother will be taken care of."

"That's too kind."

"Not really. We will be family soon. I couldn't help my brother, but I can at least help your mother."

"Thank you."

They were quiet for a moment, and in the quiet, Violet's eyelids became heavy. But Edmund broke it again.

"I've only just realized I know not your surname. It will be Langley soon enough, but I suppose I ought to know what it is now."

"It's Blakely," Violet replied softly. She almost shivered at the thought of being called Mrs. Langley but she was suddenly too tired to think about it. Violet gave Edmund a tired smile, and turned towards the window, as the black trees of the night sped by. At some point, she fell asleep, and awoke as the carriage shook with a stop. Violet pried her eyes open, and took in her dark surroundings. Her head was rested on Edmund's shoulder, most comfortably. Still, this closeness rattled her, and Violet sat up, glad the carriage was too dark so Edmund could not see her reddened cheeks. It would take time to accept their growing familiarity with each other.

"We're here," Edmund said. Violet felt his body shift as he looked down at her. She blinked, trying to make out some basic shapes in the blackness of the night. How late at night was it? Or, was it morning?

The old woman who sat across from them was gone. When had she left? Violet felt so disoriented. The last few hours felt surreal, and she was beginning to wonder what was reality and what wasn't.

Violet scrambled out of the coach and was hit with the crisp night air. The summer was slowly coming to an end, as was the warmth of the season. Still, it was refreshing.

Kently House was very different from the Langley estate. There was a little more light on the street of London than in the coach, which allowed Violet to take in her surroundings. Kently House sat on the edge of the street, tall and narrow. There was no long drive, no garden which stretched for acres. And yet, it was still magnificent. Windows with ornate trim spotted the building every few inches. Other buildings of a similar style sat closely on either side, making it difficult to determine when one home ended and another began. Edmund banged on the front door, with no response. After a few moments of silence, Edmund banged on the door again, this time yelling, "Butchman!" Finally, a man in a nightshirt opened the door, sporting a scowl and a tired grumble.

"Who could possibly be calling at this hour?" the man, presumably Butchman, muttered under his breath. He held a half-used candle up to Edmund's face. The yellow glow from the light was enough for Butchman to recognize who stood before him. "Oh! Mr. Langley! Forgive me, sir, I wasn't expecting you to arrive this early,"

Butchman stepped aside, allowing Edmund and Violet to enter. The house was dark and quiet, likely all inhabitants asleep.

"Neither was I, Butchman. I trust you've kept my house in good order while I've been away?" Edmund asked.

"Certainly,"

"If you'd be so kind, would you have the fire started in my room? Start one in the guest bedchamber that overlooks the courtyard, as well."

Butchman's eyes slid to Violet, and he looked her up and down, as if just realizing her presence. Violet could only imagine what the footman thought of her. The implications of her presence made her stomach turn, and she once again found herself grateful for the darkness, which hid her discomfort.

"Of course," Butchman said, giving Violet one last examination, before giving her a polite smile. "I'll have one of the maids do it with urgency."

"No need to wake one of the maids, when you're quite capable of starting a fire yourself." Edmund's tone was commanding, yet kind. Though Violet was used to him being her superior, it was an odd thing to see him as someone's master, giving orders.

"Uh-yes, quite, sir," Butchman said, with some hesitancy, before disappearing up a flight of stairs.

It wasn't long before Violet was settled in her room for the night. The warm flames from the fireplace lit the bedchamber enough for her to make out the subtleties of the room. She set her velise on a large wooden truck, which sat at the foot of her bed. Violet crawled into bed, which was larger than she was used to, and the sheets softer. If she wasn't so tired, Violet might have resumed her worried thoughts about the past and future, but she was exhausted, and soon fell back asleep.

*

Edmund waited in the parlor for Violet, gulping down his tea as if he had a thirst for it. When in fact, Edmund had no thirst, or appetite at all. The warm brown liquid was merely an attempt at soothing his nerves, which, Edmund reckoned, was done in vain. He refused to show any sense of feeling other than confidence around Violet. He needed to be strong for the both of them, if they were ever to heal from the prior night. Edmund had known Katherine wouldn't take the news of Edmund and Violet's relationship gracefully, but he hadn't quite expected the display she had shown.

And now, it appeared by some devious act of Judis himself, rumors of Edmund and Violet were already circulating. It made no sense at all, the whole of it, or how Katherine even discovered the two of them. But Edmund was tired of thinking about it, so he took another sip of his tea.

With a sudden wisp of muslin, Violet appeared in the doorway, looking quite striking, though in Edmund's opinion she always looked quite striking.

"Violet, good morning," he said, trying to exude an amiable countenance. Violet entered the room, and immediately began scanning the cobalt walls of the parlor. She tentatively explored the room, and while doing so, grazed her fingertips against a yellow chair that sat stationary across from Edmund. Much of the furnishings in the room were of the mustard-yellow variety. Bold patterns painted the upholstery, rugs, and curtains, all different, yet somehow cohesive. It was very unlike Alfred and Katherine Langley's parlor, which was extremely subtle and muted. But Edmund was very much unlike Alfred and Katherine.

Edmund watched, almost amused, as Violet took in her surroundings. He set down his tea and rose from his seat.

"You can change anything you'd like in Kently house when you become mistress of it. I reckon this place has been in need of a woman's touch for some time," Edmund said with a crooked smile.

"No," Violet said quickly. She turned, as if trying to take in every detail of the vibrant room. "I quite like it how it is. I had not the pleasure of seeing your home in the fullness of light when we arrived. But now I see that it is. . . cheerful." Edmund smiled, and sat back down, satisfied with Violet's answer. Violet sat down on an oriental floral chair, and smoothed her skirts in her lap, in the same anxious manor she had when they had first met.

"Tea?"

"No thank you."

"What? An English lady refusing tea? I never thought I'd see the day!" Edmund's attempt to make a joke fell flat. Violet smiled, and began twisting her fingers in her lap. The two sat in silence, avoiding what needed to be said, but neither wanting to.

"I've been trying to wrap my brain around this whole situation," Edmund started. He stared intensely into the bottom of his tea cup, watching the remaining last sip swirl around its walls. "And I cannot figure out how Katherine discovered our relationship. We were so discreet, so careful--

"I--I believe I know how."

Violet's tentative, whisper of a voice seemed to crash into Edmund like a wave. He looked up and studied her expression. Her cheeks were flushed, and she looked rather uncomfortable, in the way she kept fidgeting.

"How?" Edmund asked softly.

"A maid."

"Well, I suppose one of the servants could have seen us, but I doubt that any of them would have tattled to Katherine. Most of them are too frightened of her to even look at her, let alone share such a story." Servants were known for knowing everyone's secrets and spreading rumors among themselves, but to take it to Katherine was another thing entirely.

"Well, it was a. . .particular maid. One rather devious."

Edmund frowned, suddenly worried with what Violet might say next.

"And how do you know this particular maid was devious?"

"She, er, knew about our relationship. She saw us kiss the night of my birthday,"

"Go on,"

"She knew about us and she was extorting money from me in exchange for keeping quiet." The last bit came out in a flood of words, almost too quickly for Edmund to process what she had said. He blinked and started blankly at Violet, wondering to himself if he had really heard her correctly.

"She was blackmailing you? Judas!" Anger raged inside Edmund's stomach. He felt sick that one of his brother's maids would actually do such a thing. Violet nodded, avoiding any eye contact with him.

"Why didn't you tell me before?" Edmund squeezed his fisted into tight knots, trying to subside his sudden anger for this maid.

"You had enough to worry about, what with your brother's finances. I did not wish you to feel responsible for me as well." Violet said softly.

"You should have told me," Edmund said. He felt a twinge of disappointment in his stomach, that Violet would keep such a thing as blackmail a secret from him. Their honesty with one another was something that he had cherished.

"I'm sorry Edmund. I--I thought it for the best."

They fell silent, in an awkward wave Edmund hadn't felt with Violet in a long time. Dark circles framed her eyes and she looked paler than usual. She looked tired; more so than usual.

"It is in the past now," Edmund said. And he hoped the past was where it would stay.

Chapter Seventeen

"Miss?"

A mousy looking maid stood in the doorway, her large brown eyes filled with concern.

"Yes?"

"Might I help you dress, Miss?"

"No, thank you. That will not be necessary. I can manage myself."

"Oh." The young maid looked almost disappointed and she fidgeted with her fingers. Violet bit her lip and looked in the looking glass.

"I feel sick," she muttered to herself. Edmund was taking her to a ball that he had been invited to. His appearance was an obligation to his acquaintances of London, but Violet knew not why he insisted on bringing her along as well. She would be perfectly content staying in Kentley House, reading by a fire in solitude, while Edmund went out. She told him as much, too, but he insisted that she attend with him. Which was why Violet now felt sick.

"Shall I tell Mr. Langley you are unwell?"

"No, no, I am quite well. I'll be down in a few minutes." The maid nodded, her white-blond curls bobbing. Violet fiddled with her own hair, trying to make it look somewhat attractive. The mousy maid still stood in the doorway, looking rather unsure of herself.

"If I may, Miss," the maid started. Violet paused and looked back up at her. "You might want to plait some of your hair and pin it in the back. I reckon it's rather fashionable."

"Might you help me with my hair then? I'm afraid I have only gotten it to look pretty once this summer," Violet said, thinking back to her birthday dinner with the Langleys. That memory seemed to flood her mind often these days. The maid beamed at Violet's request for help, and she scurried over to her, likely thrilled with the chance to act as a lady's maid of sorts. Violet wasn't used to being waited on and assisted in such a way, but she could tell it brought the young girl's joy. She carefully plaited and twisted and pinned Violet's hair until it looked stunning. She wondered if this was what it was like to be wealthy. Next, the maid helped her into her evening gown. It felt nice to be back in her violet gown, as if she was reliving the happy night she and Edmund had first kissed. It was the only dress she had ever felt beautiful in, and yet something tugged at her, reminding her that tonight would be nothing like that one.

"It's as though I'm in a completely different world now. I doubt I'll fare well in London society."

"Oh, don't say that, Miss! You'll be wonderful." The mousy maid said with an innocent smile. There was something about her that put Violet at ease, and she took comfort in that feeling. She appreciated that the girl did not pry about her sudden appearance with Edmund. Why a strange, poor lady was suddenly living with Edmund Langley. Violet knew all the help must be burning with curiosity, but all this maid did was show kindness towards her. It was a welcomed change.

"Pray, what is your name?" Violet asked.

"Lilly, Miss," the maid said.

"Lilly. What a beautiful name," Violet said, testing the name out in her mouth. "I've always been fond of flowers." Lilly smiled, and gave her an unbalanced curtsy, as she was dismissed from the room. But before she left, she stopped and turned back at Violet, who was staring at herself in the looking glass.

"If I may say, Miss, I think you'll do splendid against the Londoners."

"Thank you, Lilly," Violet said with a smile. She was filled with a sudden burst of confidence for the night, though the feeling wouldn't last long.

The ballroom was crowded with voices and people. Edmund and Violet were announced, and it felt the whole world stared at them with appalled expressions, but in truth, few people paid any mind. They were too concerned with socializing themselves with the figures who had titles and importance. Still, somehow to Violet, if felt as though every critical eye was on her. With every glance she received, she feared what wicked thoughts and judgments were being made on her behalf.

"Mr. Langley, what a surprise to see you here," an older woman dripping in shining jewels said. "And is this. . .

She let her words fall off, politely asking for an introduction.

"My fiance," Edmund proclaimed. Violet tightened her grip around his arm, which was twisted against her own. "This is Violet Blakely, Ms. Blakely, this is Lady Elizabeth Summerfield."

"How marvelous, I had not known you had found yourself a match. Tell me, are you of the Hertfordshire Blakely's? Perhaps I know your father."

"I don't believe you would know him, Your Ladyship." Violet said softly. She didn't want to expand any further, but she feared she would have to. But to her surprise the woman only laughed.

"Your Ladyship?" Lady Summerfield asked in confusion. Violet's stomach dropped, and she felt her face burning. That's right, only servants would call her Ladyship.

"Lady Summerfield," Violet said, quickly correcting herself.

Several other ladies slowly joined their party, quickly exchanging polite introductions and questioning Mr. Langley on his new love.

"You look familiar, Ms. Blakely, I swear we have met before," A young woman with fiery red hair said. Her eyes looked Violet up and down, as if examining her like a piece of art. When was your Coming Out? You look about the same age as me, perhaps we came out at the same time."

"I--I didn't have a Coming Out," Violet said. Her face burned at the memory. Her father had meant her to have one, despite their place in society. But it never happened.

"You didn't have a Season in London? How odd," Lady Summerfield cried.

"Ms. Blakely's father was a clergyman, who passed away when Violet came of age." Edmund said. Everyone within earshot gasped at this statement, including Violet. How could he have just shared this detailed information about her life to these strangers?

"Your father was a clergyman?" Lady Summerfield ask, all warmth dripping from her countenance. "I was mistaken then, I would not know him."

"But I know you," the red-haired woman started. Then her eyes suddenly went wide in remembrance. "Oh of course, I remember! Some months ago I had tea with Mrs. Langley and you were in attendance!" She seemed rather content with her answer, clearly not remembering the whole of their meeting. The lady assumed Violet had been at Langley House as a guest, and Violet wasn't about to correct her.

"Yes, Ms. Blakely lived at Langley house for over two years," Edmund said. His expression was calm and firm, as if stating a fact from a history book. "She was the governess to my brother's children."

Another round of shock rippled through the party. The red-haired woman's face went paler than it's natural white color. Her face fell in true, awkward, remembrance.

"Oh yes, that's right. How lovely." She said, lacking sincerity but not politeness. Violet felt numb. Red and numb, and perhaps a little dizzy. She couldn't fathom why Edmund was exposing every scandal of her past. Did he want everyone in the ballroom to know their history?

Lady Summerfield became cold extremely quickly. Her demeanor changed from a friendly interest to utter judgment, as she realized Violet really was nothing more than a servant.

"Well, how brave of you to come," Lady Summerfield said with a smile not quite reaching her eyes. It was Mrs. Langley's signature look. "I know I would feel so uncomfortable in a place I knew I did not belong." Her words cut Violet like a knife, and she stood in a mortified silence. The others giggled wickedly but said nothing else when Edmund gave them a surn look.

"Excuse us," he said, like a vexed father, as he pulled Violet away from the crowd. "I'd like you to meet Lord Palmer."

The rest of the night seemed to repeat itself in just that way. Violet and Edmund mingled politely with the other guests, until they discovered Violet's background. As soon as they realized Mr. Langley was to marry his brother's loley governess, they spit cool remarks at them. Finally it was too much for Violet to take.

"I need some air," She said. She pulled away from Edmund's grasp and nearly bolted to the glass doors leading to the balcony. She was quickly met with a sharp, crisp breeze stroking her face as she looked out at the night sky. The loud scuffle of the ballroom was drowned out by the stillness of the night. A young couple stood closely together some yards away, at the other end of the balcony. They giggled and inched closer together, clearly enjoying the escape of a chaperone. Violet sighed in envy. It certainly was most fun to be in love when no one knew. Because if no one knew then it couldn't be ruined. It could stay a precious, beautiful gift between the couple, and nothing else would matter. How she missed that feeling.

Edmund burst through the doors and rushed to Violet's side, in a state of panic.

"You took off so quickly, I feared I had lost you!" Edmund cried. He looked relieved if only for a moment. He immediately knew something was wrong. He always knew, just by looking at her. He saw Violet more than anyone. "What is wrong, are you ill?"

"What do you think is wrong, Edmund?" Violet snapped much more harshly than she had meant to. Her harshness always seemed to surprise her these days. "How could you expect me to enjoy this night when I am so clearly out of place? And why are you telling everyone about my past? Telling everyone in London society that you plan to marry a governess, is not going to aid the situation!" Her voice grew louder with each sentence, finally letting her emotions out after a long night of restraint. Edmund furrowed his brows, as if confused by her outburst.

"Why would I not tell them? I am not going to hide who you are or lie about our past, like I am ashamed of it. Because I am not."

"But you are encouraging everyone to look at me differently! Why should I even attempt to blend into your world, when you're telling everyone I'm not from it?"

"That is not what I was doing, Violet! Surely you realise we cannot hide from the truth. Your father was a clergyman. He was a respectable man. That is nothing to be embarrassed about."

"Don't you dare insinuate that I am embarrassed by my father!"

"Well what else do you want to call it?" Edmund said, his tone had reached the elevated level that Violet's had, as both boiled with anger. They had never fought like this before, and it felt horrible. The couple on the other side of the balcony looked over at the two, startled out of their love making, and scurried back into the ballroom. The romantic atmosphere had certainly been dissipated.

"Violet, how many times do I have to tell you that I am not embarrassed by your profession, your life. I am proud of you for working hard and being the person you are."

"That is the problem, Edmund. You think everyone around us will look past my lack of wealth and standing, as you do but--

"There is nothing to look past! It is not as though you are a lady of the night!"

"Yes, Edmund, at least I'm not a prostitute. How charming you are."

"That is not what I meant," Emdund said with a sigh. He reached out to stroke Violet's arm, but she pulled away. His affections had always calmed her in the past, but for some reason she did not wish to be calmed this time. She wanted to be vexxed, and she was.

"Anyway, I reckon half of the people in that ballroom believe you are only marrying me because you've spoilt my innocence."

"Again, you reference what others might think of us. Violet, it doesn't matter what any of them think! What matters is our love and that is all. If they do not believe in our love, then they need not be in our lives."

"And then you will have lost your family, as well as your friends." Violet said, tears welling up in her eyes.

"None of those people are my friends," said Edmund. "All we should care of is our love, and that is all." His tone softened as he looked upon Violet, who refused to look back at him. Her hands tightly gripped the stone rail of the balcony, as she looked out over the grand gardens in the night. Tears silently rolled down her face, as she realized, for the first time, that she truly doubted being with Edmund.

"But is our love strong enough?" Violet cracked. She felt Edmund's pain at her words. He took a step back from her and stiffened, as if he did not recognize the woman who stood before him.

"That is a question you will have to answer. Because my love for you will not be strong enough for the both of us."

Edmund turned and walked away from her, moving back into the life of the ballroom. Their argument had ended for the night, but Violet felt it was only a matter of time before it resumed. It was all too clear now how differently they saw their love. Violet wondered, with a burning pit in her stomach, how she and Edmund could have a life together if they couldn't agree on the very basis of it.

Chapter Eighteen

Violet could not stop her mind from replaying the events of last night's ball, all through the early hours of the next morning. She felt unsettled, and rather cross with Edmund for making the night so uncomfortable. They hadn't said more than a word to one another since their argument; it was as if they were both afraid to speak to one another. But it was just as well. Violet needed time to think. She had claimed a small sitting room as her own at Kently House, where Edmund was not allowed to bother her. In a way, it reminded her of her old room at the Langley estate--small and cosy, with nothing but flowers in vases to make it beautiful.

"Ms. Blakely," Lilly called, bursting through Violet's solitude as she entered the room. Violet startled, nearly spilling the tea she was holding. She set it down with a soft giggle.

"Yes, Lilly?"

"I apologize for interrupting, but a letter just came for you," Lilly said. She held out a folded letter, crisp and white. Violet frowned, wondering who could possibly be writing to her. Even her own Mama did not yet know that she was now in London. But her heart nearly burst in understanding when her eyes studied the wax seal. It was the Langley seal, and the writing was most assuredly Mrs. Langley's.

"Thank you, Lilly," Violet said absently. Her fingers burned at the touch of the letter. She could only guess what atrocities were hidden beneath the folds of the paper. Lilly curtsied, and turned to leave, but not before bumping into the side of the doorway. She clumsily steadied herself, almost knocking over a nearby vase of flowers in the process.

"Oh!" Lilly shrieked. She outreached her arms and clutched the vase, holding it carefully in her hands before ensuring its safety back on the side table. The spectacle was enough to make Violet smile, if only for a moment.

She took a deep breath, and mustered every courage she had to break the seal and read Mrs. Langley's words. Perhaps, by the divinity of God, Mrs. Langley's words would actually be good. Perhaps, she would confess that she had reacted harshly. Perhaps not.

Dear Violet,

As you left with Mr. Langley, I can only assume he took you to his home in London, which is where I have sent this letter to. I can only hope, at least, that is where he took you, and not Scotland.....

Of course, Mrs. Langley feared Edmund had whisked her away to Gretna Green to marry.

.....I am not one to pretend pleasantries when none are present. I cannot be insincere, in all my faults, that is surely one you can respect in me. I will admit that a large part of my disapproval comes for your inequality. You and Mr. Langley are from two different worlds, and as such, your relationship is entirely inappropriate in my eyes. And for it to blossom, if you will, under my home, was an even larger blow. But none of this you doubt, I am sure, so I will tell you my other reasonings. I do not know what Mr. Langley has told you of my husband's financial issues. But if you are as intelligent as I believe you to be, you will know that my Alfred has found himself in rather dire gambling debts. It is not easy for me to admit, but it is my family's shame to bear.

What I doubt you know is that the man, Lord Albey, to whom my husband owes money, is of close relation to Ms. Hart. She is to inherit all of his fortune, and collect monies from his indebtors. Lord Albey has recently given your Mr. Langley a chance to mend these debts. By marrying Ms. Hart, Lord Albey will waive all debts owed by my husband. My family will be saved from ruin. And my children, whom I know you love dearly, will continue to live a good life, with solid places in society.

I ask you to let go of Edmund Langley not for my benefit or disapproval, but for the well-being of the children, and the Langley family. Alfred and Edmund Langley have always had a difficult relationship, but I fear this fracture, if it continues, will tear them apart forever. I know I behaved badly, but my husband is more forgiving than I am. Surely he must not suffer for my poor behavior. Neither should dearest Charlotte and Fredric, who would be forced out of their family home for ever.

I know you are a good person, Violet, despite your follies. And because of this, I trust you will make the right decision. If you do release Mr. Langley, I will give you a shining letter of recommendation, so you may take another position as a governess, and keep your livelihood.

Respectively,

K. Langley

Violet read and reread the letter, each time with a heavier sense of dread then the last. It was the most civil Mrs. Langley had ever been to her. And while she was certain that the separation for her and Edmund would delight Mrs. Langley for selfish reasons, Violet could not deny that she made a sound argument. She had been unaware of Edmund's offer from

Lord Albey. He could save his family. Though Mrs. Langley did not deserve saving, he could still repay the kindness that Alfred had given him in Oxford, despite his flaws. And there were the children. Before Violet had left the Langley estate, she was under the impression that Edmund could do nothing more to try and save his family's fortune. But that wasn't the case.

Violet took in several cups of tea as she mulled over her thoughts. She would always feel out of place in such a marriage, she knew that now more than ever. She wasn't a great lady; her past would always ensure that much. Even though Edmund was a younger brother who would spend his life in work, he was still of a higher station and class, and always would be. No matter how many times Edmund claimed it didn't matter, she knew it would. Who knew how many years of marriage and children would it take before it finally tore them apart.

Mrs. Langley's letter might not have stabbed at Violet's heart the way it did, had it not been for the previous night. Reality was beginning to crash over her in large waves, each blow colder and more sobering than the last. As much has she hated it, Violet felt a beckoning of what she knew was right. She rang for Lilly, who scrambled into the sitting room, ready to report for duty.

"Lilly, please call for the coach, and pack my things. I would do it myself, but I can't bare risking the chance of seeing Mr. Langley." Violet commanded. She fought back tears as she spoke. Lilly's face fell, knowing what this meant.

"Are, are you certain, Miss?"

"Yes, I am quite certain."

Lilly nodded and disappeared, leaving Violet to wait silently once more. It did not take long for everything to be settled, but it felt like an eternity.

Violet stood and watched out the window as a coach arrived out front. A footman carried her vellise out to it, ready to strap it on top of the carriage. Violet swallowed, but a large lump of sorrow caught in her throat. It was time then.

Just as she reached to open the door of her sitting room, it flung out on its own. Edmund stood in her way, his eyes wide with concern.

"Where are you going, Violet? I've been informed that a coach is out front waiting for you."

"I'm leaving," Violet cracked. "To be with my Mama." Her heart was filled with pain as she watched Edmund's expression twist into concern. He furrowed his brows and reached out to touch her hands.

"I don't understand. You are leaving without me?" Edmund asked. Violet averted her eyes and took a deep breath.

"I am. I am leaving, Edmund, and I am not coming back," she said.

"What are you speaking of? What has brought you to this?" Edmund asked. He held on tighter to Violet's hands, as if she would slip away any minute.

"I have realized that I have been selfish and unrealistic in my love for you. I will never fit in your world, and you will surely regret giving it up for me. I am freeing you from being bound to me before either of us can regret marriage."

"I would never regret marrying you," Edmund cried.

"You say that now, but what of five years from now? Are you really willing to give up your family for me? Your reputation?"

"Of course I am! Have my intentions not been entirely clear? Violet from the first moment I laid eyes on you I was willing to lose everything for you."

"But I'm not willing to let you. You might not care that our relationship has caused the estrangement of what little family you have left. That we're a scandal story in your circle of society. And my conscience won't allow me to not care." It took everything Violet had not to crumble to the floor in sobs. It pained her to leave him, to see his own pain which she inflicted. Edmund's hands sank to the sides of his body, and tightened into balls.

"You know, you're no better than Katherine, you know that? Your chief concerns have always been about what other people might think, when the truth is, all that should matter is what you think. Do you love me? It is as simple as that."

"What I think is that it is not as simple as that. My love for you, and for your niece and nephew,is why I must leave. You have a chance to marry Ms. Hart and save your family fortune, so that Charlotte and Fredric may have a good life. And you may rebuild your family's name with a respectable wife. But with me by your side, that will never happen."

"How to you know of Ms. Hart?"

"Mrs. Langley wrote to me."

"Well that explains it!" Edmund spat, his voice angered in his pain. "Do not fall for her manipulation! Mrs. Langley has known about the debts for some time now, and she is selfishly manipulating those around her to get what she wants!"

"It is no matter! It makes no difference, for she is right!" Viold cried, with an equal amount of passion. She broke away from Edmund and paced backwards. Tears welled in her eyes as she spoke.

"I do not accept it," Edmund said.

"You must, as I have," said Violet. She squeezed her eyes to prevent tears from falling down her cheeks. Edmund turns his back towards Violet, but still he blocked the doorway. They stood silent for a few moments, Violet trying to mask her tears and sniffles, and Edmund doing the same. Finally he turned to look at her with tears in his eyes. All anger had gone from his expression, and when he spoke, his voice was soft and defeated.

"Perhaps you are correct. For, no matter how many times I tell you how much you're worth everything to me, you will never believe me. Not until you believe it for yourself. You think so little of yourself and so much of everyone around you. And I'm finished trying to convince you otherwise."

"Good," was all Violet managed to say. Edmund's words hung over her and stung like a wasp. "This is for the best. I'm releasing you from your obligations to me."

"You were never an obligation," He said. Finally, Edmund side stepped and held the door open, motioning for Violet to leave.

"Goodbye, Mr. Langley," Violet whispered, managing a small curtsy, before nearly bolting out the door. She didn't allow herself to look back as she made her way out to the coach. She didn't think she could bear watching Edmund as she left him. It would be too easy to change her mind and run back to him. But Violet knew she couldn't. Instead, she climbed in the coach and pounded her fist into the ceiling, telling the driver to go.

*

It was a long dive home. Though Violet had left London in the morning, it was nightfall by the time she made it to her mama's village. She didn't bother knocking when she reached the small cottage, which sat on the edge of the road which led to the center of the village.

Violet dropped her vellise on the scuffed floor as Mrs. Blakely scurried around the corner in her nightdress. She held a very well-used candle at eye-level as she squinted through the darkness at her daughter.

"What on earth?" Mrs. Blakely said. "Dear Violet, is that you?"

"Mama?" Violet squeaked. It was all she could say before she collapsed into her mother's arms in wild sobs. Being at her Mama's cottage, Violet felt a sudden finality. She likely would never see Edmund Langley ever again. She would never feel the touch of his strong, gentle hands, or feel his kind gaze on her skin. It truly was over now, yet still her heart hurt from loving him.

The past was to be left where history lied, where memories of her deceased father hid, and where honeysuckle kisses would be forgotten.

For much of the night, Violet felt the comfort of her mother's strong, warm embrace. She felt like a child again, seeking that maternal touch, which would hold her together and reassure her everything would be well in time. Mrs. Blakey didn't ask her what had happened, which Violet was grateful for. It didn't matter; what mattered were the large tears that fell down Violet's cheeks and which wet her mother's tattered nightdress. Tears that flowed like a heavy rainstorm, which would not slow until the darkened cloud was gone.

Chapter Nineteen

Violet could not stop her mind from replaying the events of last night's ball, all through the early hours of the next morning. She felt unsettled, and rather cross with Edmund for making the night so uncomfortable. They hadn't said more than a word to one another since their argument; it was as if they were both afraid to speak to one another. But it was just as well. Violet needed time to think. She had claimed a small sitting room as her own at Kently House, where Edmund was not allowed to bother her. In a way, it reminded her of her old room at the Langley estate--small and cosy, with nothing but flowers in vases to make it beautiful.

"Ms. Blakely," Lilly called, bursting through Violet's solitude as she entered the room. Violet startled, nearly spilling the tea she was holding. She set it down with a soft giggle.

"Yes, Lilly?"

"I apologize for interrupting, but a letter just came for you," Lilly said. She held out a folded letter, crisp and white. Violet frowned, wondering who could possibly be writing to her. Even her own Mama did not yet know that she was now in London. But her heart nearly burst in understanding when her eyes studied the wax seal. It was the Langley seal, and the writing was most assuredly Mrs. Langley's.

"Thank you, Lilly," Violet said absently. Her fingers burned at the touch of the letter. She could only guess what atrocities were hidden beneath the folds of the paper. Lilly curtsied, and turned to leave, but not before bumping into the side of the doorway. She clumsily steadied herself, almost knocking over a nearby vase of flowers in the process.

"Oh!" Lilly shrieked. She outreached her arms and clutched the vase, holding it carefully in her hands before ensuring its safety back on the side table. The spectacle was enough to make Violet smile, if only for a moment.

She took a deep breath, and mustered every courage she had to break the seal and read Mrs. Langley's words. Perhaps, by the divinity of God, Mrs. Langley's words would actually be good. Perhaps, she would confess that she had reacted harshly. Perhaps not.

Dear Violet,

As you left with Mr. Langley, I can only assume he took you to his home in London, which is where I have sent this letter to. I can only hope, at least, that is where he took you, and not Scotland.....

Of course, Mrs. Langley feared Edmund had whisked her away to Gretna Green to marry.

.....I am not one to pretend pleasantries when none are present. I cannot be insincere, in all my faults, that is surely one you can respect in me. I will admit that a large part of my disapproval comes for your inequality. You and Mr. Langley are from two different worlds, and as such, your relationship is entirely inappropriate in my eyes. And for it to blossom, if you will, under my home, was an even larger blow. But none of this you doubt, I am sure, so I will tell you my other reasonings. I do not know what Mr. Langley has told you of my husband's financial issues. But if you are as intelligent as I believe you to be, you will know that my Alfred has found himself in rather dire gambling debts. It is not easy for me to admit, but it is my family's shame to bear.

What I doubt you know is that the man, Lord Albey, to whom my husband owes money, is of close relation to Ms. Hart. She is to inherit all of his fortune, and collect monies from his indebtors. Lord Albey has recently given your Mr. Langley a chance to mend these debts. By marrying Ms. Hart, Lord Albey will waive all debts owed by my husband. My family will be saved from ruin. And my children, whom I know you love dearly, will continue to live a good life, with solid places in society.

I ask you to let go of Edmund Langley not for my benefit or disapproval, but for the well-being of the children, and the Langley family. Alfred and Edmund Langley have always had a difficult relationship, but I fear this fracture, if it continues, will tear them apart forever. I know I behaved badly, but my husband is more forgiving than I am. Surely he must not suffer for my poor behavior. Neither should dearest Charlotte and Fredric, who would be forced out of their family home for ever.

I know you are a good person, Violet, despite your follies. And because of this, I trust you will make the right decision. If you do release Mr. Langley, I will give you a shining letter of recommendation, so you may take another position as a governess, and keep your livelihood.

Respectively,

K. Langley

Violet read and reread the letter, each time with a heavier sense of dread then the last. It was the most civil Mrs. Langley had ever been to her. And while she was certain that the separation for her and Edmund would delight Mrs. Langley for selfish reasons, Violet could not deny that she made a sound argument. She had been unaware of Edmund's offer from

Lord Albey. He could save his family. Though Mrs. Langley did not deserve saving, he could still repay the kindness that Alfred had given him in Oxford, despite his flaws. And there were the children. Before Violet had left the Langley estate, she was under the impression that Edmund could do nothing more to try and save his family's fortune. But that wasn't the case.

Violet took in several cups of tea as she mulled over her thoughts. She would always feel out of place in such a marriage, she knew that now more than ever. She wasn't a great lady; her past would always ensure that much. Even though Edmund was a younger brother who would spend his life in work, he was still of a higher station and class, and always would be. No matter how many times Edmund claimed it didn't matter, she knew it would. Who knew how many years of marriage and children would it take before it finally tore them apart.

Mrs. Langley's letter might not have stabbed at Violet's heart the way it did, had it not been for the previous night. Reality was beginning to crash over her in large waves, each blow colder and more sobering than the last. As much has she hated it, Violet felt a beckoning of what she knew was right. She rang for Lilly, who scrambled into the sitting room, ready to report for duty.

"Lilly, please call for the coach, and pack my things. I would do it myself, but I can't bare risking the chance of seeing Mr. Langley." Violet commanded. She fought back tears as she spoke. Lilly's face fell, knowing what this meant.

"Are, are you certain, Miss?"

"Yes, I am quite certain."

Lilly nodded and disappeared, leaving Violet to wait silently once more. It did not take long for everything to be settled, but it felt like an eternity.

Violet stood and watched out the window as a coach arrived out front. A footman carried her vellise out to it, ready to strap it on top of the carriage. Violet swallowed, but a large lump of sorrow caught in her throat. It was time then.

Just as she reached to open the door of her sitting room, it flung out on its own. Edmund stood in her way, his eyes wide with concern.

"Where are you going, Violet? I've been informed that a coach is out front waiting for you."

"I'm leaving," Violet cracked. "To be with my Mama." Her heart was filled with pain as she watched Edmund's expression twist into concern. He furrowed his brows and reached out to touch her hands.

"I don't understand. You are leaving without me?" Edmund asked. Violet averted her eyes and took a deep breath.

"I am. I am leaving, Edmund, and I am not coming back," she said.

"What are you speaking of? What has brought you to this?" Edmund asked. He held on tighter to Violet's hands, as if she would slip away any minute.

"I have realized that I have been selfish and unrealistic in my love for you. I will never fit in your world, and you will surely regret giving it up for me. I am freeing you from being bound to me before either of us can regret marriage."

"I would never regret marrying you," Edmund cried.

"You say that now, but what of five years from now? Are you really willing to give up your family for me? Your reputation?"

"Of course I am! Have my intentions not been entirely clear? Violet from the first moment I laid eyes on you I was willing to lose everything for you."

"But I'm not willing to let you. You might not care that our relationship has caused the estrangement of what little family you have left. That we're a scandal story in your circle of society. And my conscience won't allow me to not care." It took everything Violet had not to crumble to the floor in sobs. It pained her to leave him, to see his own pain which she inflicted. Edmund's hands sank to the sides of his body, and tightened into balls.

"You know, you're no better than Katherine, you know that? Your chief concerns have always been about what other people might think, when the truth is, all that should matter is what you think. Do you love me? It is as simple as that."

"What I think is that it is not as simple as that. My love for you, and for your niece and nephew, is why I must leave. You have a chance to marry Ms. Hart and save your family fortune, so that Charlotte and Fredric may have a good life. And you may rebuild your family's name with a respectable wife. But with me by your side, that will never happen."

"How to you know of Ms. Hart?"

"Mrs. Langley wrote to me."

"Well that explains it!" Edmund spat, his voice angered in his pain. "Do not fall for her manipulation! Mrs. Langley has known about the debts for some time now, and she is selfishly manipulating those around her to get what she wants!"

"It is no matter! It makes no difference, for she is right!" Viold cried, with an equal amount of passion. She broke away from Edmund and paced backwards. Tears welled in her eyes as she spoke.

"I do not accept it," Edmund said.

"You must, as I have," said Violet. She squeezed her eyes to prevent tears from falling down her cheeks. Edmund turns his back towards Violet, but still he blocked the doorway. They stood silent for a few moments, Violet trying to mask her tears and sniffles, and Edmund doing the same. Finally he turned to look at her with tears in his eyes. All anger had gone from his expression, and when he spoke, his voice was soft and defeated.

"Perhaps you are correct. For, no matter how many times I tell you how much you're worth everything to me, you will never believe me. Not until you believe it for yourself. You think so little of yourself and so much of everyone around you. And I'm finished trying to convince you otherwise."

"Good," was all Violet managed to say. Edmund's words hung over her and stung like a wasp. "This is for the best. I'm releasing you from your obligations to me."

"You were never an obligation," He said. Finally, Edmund side stepped and held the door open, motioning for Violet to leave.

"Goodbye, Mr. Langley," Violet whispered, managing a small curtsy, before nearly bolting out the door. She didn't allow herself to look back as she made her way out to the coach. She didn't think she could bear watching Edmund as she left him. It would be too easy to change her mind and run back to him. But Violet knew she couldn't. Instead, she climbed in the coach and pounded her fist into the ceiling, telling the driver to go.

*

It was a long dive home. Though Violet had left London in the morning, it was nightfall by the time she made it to her mama's village. She didn't bother knocking when she reached the small cottage, which sat on the edge of the road which led to the center of the village.

Violet dropped her vellise on the scuffed floor as Mrs. Blakely scurried around the corner in her nightdress. She held a very well-used candle at eye-level as she squinted through the darkness at her daughter.

"What on earth?" Mrs. Blakely said. "Dear Violet, is that you?"

"Mama?" Violet squeaked. It was all she could say before she collapsed into her mother's arms in wild sobs. Being at her Mama's cottage, Violet felt a sudden finality. She likely would never see Edmund Langley ever again. She would never feel the touch of his strong, gentle hands, or feel his kind gaze on her skin. It truly was over now, yet still her heart hurt from loving him.

The past was to be left where history lied, where memories of her deceased father hid, and where honeysuckle kisses would be forgotten.

For much of the night, Violet felt the comfort of her mother's strong, warm embrace. She felt like a child again, seeking that maternal touch, which would hold her together and reassure her everything would be well in time. Mrs. Blakey didn't ask her what had happened, which Violet was grateful for. It didn't matter; what mattered were the large tears that fell down Violet's cheeks and which wet her mother's tattered nightdress. Tears that flowed like a heavy rainstorm, which would not slow until the darkened cloud was gone.

Chapter Twenty

SIX MONTHS LATER

Violet ran through the garden, gripping her muslin skirts with tight fists. Its hem hovered scandalously high over her ankles, but such was necessary when running. A little girl weaved around trimmed hedges and flowers in front of her. She was surprisingly fast for a child of only three. Her giggles and squeals drifted through the air and sung in Violet's ears, causing her to giggle just as much.

"I will catch you, Elisabeth!" Violet laughed. The little girl darted behind a large elm tree, disappearing behind the thick trunk. Violet did not slow her pace as she approached the tree, wrapping her hand around it. Her fingers scraped against the rough bark.

Violet caught up to Elisabeth, whose bright orange girls gleamed in the sunlight. She reached for the girl, trying to tag her arm, but Elisabeth yelped and swerved away. Violet lurched forward, now unsteady, and collided with a large tree root. Her left ankle twisted as she collapsed to the ground, and she cried out in pain.

Elisabeth stopped short and stared for a moment at her playmate, slightly confused.

"Are you alright Ms. Violet?" she asked in a decidedly small voice. Violet clutched at her foot, trying to blink away tears. Her stocking was ripped from the fall, and she likely had scrapes on her leg from falling against the bark. But it was her ankle that swelled with sharp, stabbing pains.

"My ankle hurts immensely. Will you fetch your Mama?" Violet said in between steady breaths. Elisabeth nodded and sprinted toward the main house. Soon her Mama arrived, bunching her pale eyebrows with concern. Her red hair shined in the sunlight, much like her daughters, but it was a deeper, auburn color. Violet had never imagined the red-haired woman from the London ball would have hired her as a governess, but she did. She was a kind-hearted mistress, who always showed concern for her, which was something Violet had never received from Mrs. langley.

"Ms. Violet, you are hurt! Oh dear, I shall have one of the servants fetch the doctor," she said, crouching down to Violet, who was still draped on the ground.

"That isn't necessary, Mrs. Stevens, thank you. I'm certain with your assistance I will be able to stand and walk off the pain."

"Somehow I doubt that, dear," Mrs. Stevens replied with a soft smile. "I am sure Elisabeth will want you healed as quickly as possible, so you might play that delightful chase game of yours. And that must be done by the hands of a doctor."

Despite this speech, she complied, and attempted to pull Violet up, holding her in a tight grip by the arms. However, with even the slightest weight put on her left ankle, Violet yelped and collapsed back onto the ground.

"Perhaps I need a doctor," Violet sighed in defeat.

"Splendid! I shall have him fetched," Mrs. Stevens said, a little too happily. "It has been so very long since anyone needed a doctor, I daresay. We have been entirely too healthy here at Southsmith Park."

Mrs. Stevens found a male servant strong enough to carry Violet back inside. He rested her on the sofa in the drawing room to wait for the doctor's aid.

"Are you certain you should not want me in my bedchamber? I feel terrible for taking over your drawing room." Violet said, as Mrs. Stevens fluffed a pillow for her back. It felt rather odd for her employer to treat her so well, to service her in such a way. But that was Mrs. Stevens--caring to her core.

"Nonsense, you will have more natural sunlight in here." Mrs. Stevens said with a smile. Her eyes caught movement through the window, and her smile broadened. "The doctor is here. He will fix you right up, I am certain." She disappeared for a moment, leaving Violet alone in the drawing room.

"Our governess has fallen and twisted her ankle quite badly."

Violet could hear Mrs. Stevens just outside the door, though her voice was muffled.

"Please, lead the way to her. I will take a look," A deep, male voice said. It was oddly familiar, but through the door, Violet couldn't quite place it.

And then, the white door opened, and there he was.

Edmund Langley.

His face paled as his dark eyes fixed on her, and he stopped in his tracks. Violet's stomach twisted and her heart pounded as they stared at one another. There was something about him that looked different from when she last saw him. Could he be taller? No. Perhaps it was his hair, which had grown longer and now framed his eyes in dark curls.

"Ms. Blakely," Edmund finally said, in a cracked whisper.

"Oh, I had forgotten you two are acquainted," Mrs. Stevens said, but somehow Violet doubted that. When Mrs. Stevens had hired Violet six months ago, she knew Violet had broken her engagement with Edmund. Though time had passed since then, it seemed unlikely she would have forgotten.

"Yes, indeed, we are," Violet said. She looked down at her hands and fiddled with them, trying to hide her newly reddened face.

"Well, I will leave you to her examination, Dr. Langley." Mrs. Stevens said. Violet could have sworn she winked at her before closing the door firmly shut behind her. Gingers were quite cheeky, weren't they?

"You are a proper physician now; I shall give you my congratulations," Violet said. She hoped her tone alluded to that of casual politeness, and that Edmund could not hear how hard her heart was pounding, or how loud it was screaming.

"Thank you," Edmund replied. His eyes stayed pointedly fixed on Violet's ankle, which he bent over to inspect. "May I examine you?"

Violet nodded, but gasped when his fingers touched her skin. Edmund pulled away, clearly fearing his touch had hurt her. And though it had, Violet's discomfort was not from her ankle, but by the memories that his touch held.

"Did that hurt?"

"A little."

Edmund returned to her ankle, and with an even lighter touch, slipped off her shoe. His hands hovered over her foot for a moment, as if hesitating, before slowly pulling Violet's stocking down and dropping it on the floor.

Violet gribbed the edge of the sofa cousin and squeezed as hard as she could.

His index finger and thumb gently massaged her ankle bone, and he furrowed his brows in concentration as he assessed what he felt.

"May I ask how you came to injure yourself?" Edmund asked. He was all professional, all doctor, except in his eyes, which told a different story.

"I was running with Elisabeth and tripped," Violet replied. To her surprise, Edmund let himself smile as he looked back at her.

"Will you never learn that playing such chasing games will always end in trouble?" he laughed. Certainly he was thinking back to the first day they had met.

"I never learn anything, I'm afraid, Dr. Langley." Violet allowed herself to smile gently.

"Well I am certain that is not true."

Edmund's fingers tickled Violet's swollen skin. She felt so many feelings seeing him again. Pain, at first, at the remembrance of what had transpired between them. But also a small burst of felicity--that she did indeed get to see him again, feel his touch, receive his smile. It gave her a taste of what was, when they lived in a cloud of reverie, imagining what might be instead of what was.

What could've been their future. What might have happened if Violet had never left London. But enough of that, there was no changing the past.

"Well, I can say with certainty you have in fact sprained your ankle. You must rest and stay off your feet until it heals. And take ice baths, as the cold will help with swelling."

Edmund rose and straightened his coat, signalling the end of his examination. Something in Violet stung as the thought of him leaving so quickly. She had tucked away her feeling for him to tightly inside herself, but now they were all unravelling.

"I expect you and Ms. Hart are happy together?" Violet asked. It was intrusive and thoughtless, but she had to know. Edmund stopped at the door and turned back at her.

"Ms. Hart is now Lady Hughburt, and yes she is very happy with her new husband. But together we are not."

"Oh." That had been a strangely satisfying answer, despite the fact that Violet had initially told Emdund to marry Ms. Hart.

"I reckon I will never marry," Edmund continued. This time, his dark eyes stayed firmly fixed to Violet's. In those black eyes she saw his pain, and something else.

"And your family, how are they?"

"They will survive. They are living humbly in a cottage in Bath. I think it is for the best."

"Good," Violet said, but she didn't feel it. In all their trouble, Ms. Hart married another man, the Langleys lost their estate, and Edmund and Violet were not together. It suddenly felt as though it was all for naught.

"And you have made amends with Mr. and Mrs. Langley?"

"My brother, at least. Though I am not certain I can ever fully trust either." Edmund moved back to the door and rested his hand on the knob. "I hope you are happy, Violet."

His use of her Christain name sent riddles of warmth down her spine. Edmund left before Violet could say anything in reply, bumping into Mrs. Stevens, who had been curiously close to the drawing room door. Her mistress scurried in the room and sat in a chair near the softa. She sported a satisfied smirk, which brightened her pale face.

"He hopes you are happy, how charming," Mrs. Stevens said, her eyes sparkling.

"How much of our conversation did you overhear, if I might ask?"

"Oh, this and that. Well, mostly all of it," she admitted. "You know, when I met you first at the ball in London, I could so clearly see how much Dr. Langley adored you. Even still, he loves you, and I am certain he would have you if you gave him a little encouragement."

"Mrs. Stevens!" Violet felt her face reddening at the thought.

"I am only speaking the truth! I would be sorry to not have you as a governess for Elisabeth, but you cannot pretend you no longer love each other."

"It was never a matter of not loving one another," Violet whispered. "Though I have tried to stop loving him, I daresay you cannot choose to stop loving someone by will."

"Indeed. Yet so many of your obstacles for not being together have seemed to fade away. Surely even Mrs. Langley would accept your union now, with the hope of saving the Langley estate gone. I don't believe a woman living in a small cottage with one servant can judge a man for marrying a governess any longer." Mrs. Stevens said with a scoff.

"What are you suggesting, Mrs. Stevens?"

"That you encourage Dr. Langley enough for him to ask you for your hand. Anyone with a little sense can see that is what both of you want."

"I hardly think I could be so bold!" Violet cried, though the suggestion was tempting. Violet didn't quite know what to think; so many emotions swirled in her heart and in her mind. Seeing Edmund so unexpectedly had stirred up feelings that she had hidden so well for six months. But after all this time, was there truly enough hope for them to restart?

"Give it a thought," Mrs. Stevens said, patting Violet's hands. "But do allow yourself to be happy, whatever that might look like."

Chapter Twenty-One

A fortnight had passed since Violet and Emdund had last seen each other. In that time, Violet had restlessly considered Mrs. Steven's words. Her ankle had finally healed, so she could walk again, but running games were not quite back in her daily regiment. In this period of healing, Violet's thoughts were consumed by Edmund. She had never stopped loving him, and reckoned she never would. Though she was happy at Southsmith Park--Mr. and Mrs. Stevens were much too kind to her, and she adored little Elisabeth--she realised she had no future there. Her work as a governess, which she had once accepted to be her life, and reecepted some months ago--would never truly be enough for Violet live fully. Without Edmund, a piece of her would always be missing, empty, even.

It was long overdue to make her own happiness, and a life and a love that she had convinced she would never be worthy of, or accepted to have. It was a sudden feeling, of hope, and love, not only for Edmund, but for herself. The feeling sunk into her, spreading warmth and tingles of joy as it filled her heart.

Violet had finally felt what Edmund had been telling her everyday of their acquaintance. That she was worthy of true happiness. It was something she had known in her head, but never quite felt. After her father died, duty and place came before happiness. Family love came before romantic love. But it was time to finally hold what was meant to be hers.

*

Edmund swallowed hard to prevent his heart from leaping out of his throat. He had received a letter from Southsmith Park that he was needed urgently, and to come right away. There had been no explanation as to what was wrong, which caused his imagination to run rampant. Of course his thoughts were on Violet-- what if she had fallen down the stairs and hit her head, trying to walk on her ankle too soon? Or what if she had somehow caught an infection or illness, and she was lying in bed, dying? Or perhaps it was not Violet at all. But something in his gut told him it was.

Edmund galloped his horse through the forest, gripping his massive steed as they made their way closer to Southsmith Park. Closer to Violet.

It had taken every bit of restraint in him not to hold her in his arms and declare his love for her once more. To try again, just once, in the hopes that they might find their way back to each other. But it wasn't the time or the place to do so. And for the last fortnight he had been trying to find a way to bring about such a time or place.

But now was no time for that. Edmund rode up to the estate and jumped down from his horse. He didn't even wait for the stablehand to take the reins before he approached the front door. When he was welcomed inside, his chest nearly burst as his eyes searched for Violet, but he did not see her.

"Dr. Langley, so good of you to come. And so promptly." Mrs. Stevens said, rising from her chair in the drawing room.

"How can I be of service?" Edmund asked, still breathing heavily from the ride over.

"Ms. Blakely is in the back gardens and is in need of your assistance again." Something about Mrs. Steven's countenance seemed odd, but he paid no mind to it. He might have noticed the sparkle in her eye and the slight upwards curl in the corner of mouth--if his attentions were not so solely focused on Violet. He nodded, and allowed himself to be guided to the gardens by a footman.

Outside, the sky was darkening, as it was now evening. It turned and tinted everything in sight in a blanket of grey. All fear relaxed when Edmund's eyes landed on Violet, standing in the center of the pathway. In her hands she held a cluster of honeysuckle blossoms, their thin yellow petals almost glowing. He wanted to run to her, but somehow his feet refused to move. Instead, Violet strode up to him, stopping short only a few inches from him. She stretched her neck and looked sweetly up at him, as strands of her hair carelessly hung where they wished. She looked more beautiful and radiant than she ever had before.

"You nearly killed me," Edmund breathed. "With that letter, I thought something terrible had happened to you."

"I didn't mean to upset you," Violet said, eyes filled with concern. "But I needed to see you urgently."

"Did you?"

"Yes, because I've realized I cannot go a single day longer without telling you how much I regret leaving you at Kently House. I left a piece of myself with you that day, and I've come to tell you I'd like you to have all the rest. Because the truth is, I will love you until my dying breath." Tears welled in Violet's eyes, not from sadness, but from the wave of love and hope that radiated from her. "And I know it's rather improper of me to speak so freely, but I reckon we have never been all that proper, and there is no use starting now."

Violet held up the honeysuckle, and Edmund wordless left bent his head to smell the sweet fragrant smell of the flower. Spring had come again, and with it, a new chance to bloom.

*

Violet nuzzled her nose near Edmund's as they smelled the honeysuckle together.

And then, their eyes met.

In one look, it was as though Violet had awoken from a long, strange sleep. Gone were the days of secret dreams, imagining what life might be like with Edmund. Gone were the nightmares of their obstacles. Both were awake and ready for the life ahead, which would live together.

THE END